SO-AFM-936

Immortal Devices (A Steampunk Scarlett Novel #2)

Immortal Devices: A Steampunk Scarlett Novel
Published by THE EDGE
THE EDGE is an imprint of Sparklesoup Inc.
Copyright © 2012 Kailin Gow

For information, please contact:
THE EDGE at Sparklesoup
14252 Culver Dr., A732
Irvine, CA 92604
www.sparklesoup.com
First Edition.
Printed in the United States of America.

ISBN: 9781597480116

3

DEDICATION

For anyone who has ever been foolishly in
love...

Immortal Devices

A Steampunk Scarlett Novel

Book Two

kailin gow

1

Kailin Gow

Prologue

Scarlett sat in the dining room of her family's London home, eating a breakfast that had been brought through by her maid, Frances. The young woman had arrived back from the country just this morning with several of the other staff, and currently seemed to be determined to make up for not having been there when Scarlett arrived by not letting her do anything for herself. Already, she had insisted on helping Scarlett dress in a simple dress of bright blue that went with Scarlett's eyes, and put her blonde locks up in an elaborate arrangement that Scarlett had barely had the patience to sit there for.

The breakfast almost made up for it, though it was ludicrous, having to put up with the formality of a fully set dinner table even when breakfasting alone. Scarlett sighed. It was 1895, with the dawn of a new century near the corner. There shouldn't be such formality. Formality got in the way of practicality...a trait she picked up from her famous Egyptologist parents, and a trait emphasized by her parents' detective friend Holmes. Still, at least the tea was well made, the servants having long since learned how important it was to Scarlett. She sat there and sipped it, working her way through the food on the table methodically.

One of the broadsheets sat to one side, but there was little in it to catch Scarlett's interest after the events of the previous evening. In a world full of secret orders and magical Devices, not to mention vampires bent on exploiting those Devices for their own ends, the news that the Empire was in discussions with Germany about reorganizing some of their African territories hardly seemed that important.

Scarlett sighed. She supposed most young women her age in London society would have been happy for an adventure like the one of the last few days to be over. They would have at least welcomed the opportunity to sit down and relax after days and nights spent investigating. They would not have been sitting there, tapping out an irritated pattern on the tablecloth with their fingertips in a way that would almost certainly have drawn a sharp word from her mother had she been there.

Of course, they presumably would not have felt quite so hemmed in by what passed for normal life. They would not have felt, as Scarlett had felt when Frances helped her to prepare for the day, that they were somehow being readied for a part playing the role of the dutiful young woman. What would her day include today? Visiting one of the families she knew in London? Reading some "improving" book or other? After yesterday, it hardly seemed like enough to fill the time.

Scarlett was still sitting there contemplating that when a knock came at the door. She resisted the urge to leap up and see who it was out of sheer boredom. After all, it was not done for well off young ladies to answer their own doors. Instead, she waited as patiently as she could while Frances hurried off to answer it, muttering darkly

7

about people who called on others so early in the day, rather than at the usual hours for visiting.

It did not take long for Scarlett to detect the sounds of an argument, and less than a minute after that, a figure came barging into the room, pursued by Frances. He was a more than familiar figure, from his long, jet black hair to the slightly tanned skin and strong features that made him more than handsome. Scarlett had looked into those Kohl lined green eyes just yesterday, after all. She had stared into them, and even kissed their owner's full lips, getting a vision from doing so in a way that she still wasn't sure she fully understood. It had been a good kiss, too. Perhaps a day ago, that thought might have made Scarlett blush. She did not now. She straighten her back. The kiss was necessary to help her see into Tavian's memories. Along with her gift of seeing the supernatural, she had discovered other gifts these last few days. The one involving the ability to see the handsome gypsy Tavian's memories through a kiss was an useful and quite pleasant one, she had to admit.

"Tavian."

"You know this gypsy, Miss Scarlett?" Frances asked with obvious concern. "He pushed his way right past me, demanding to see you."

"Thank you, Frances," Scarlett said with careful restraint as she stood. Would it make any difference to the maid if she knew that Tavian was not just a passing gypsy, but also one of the magical fey, left as a changeling after birth? No, probably not. "That will be all for now."

"You want me to leave you alone in the room with this young man?" Frances sounded almost incredulous.

"That will be *all*, thank you, Frances."

The maid hurried out, and for a moment, Tavian and Scarlett stood there looking at one another.

"Tavian," Scarlett asked, "is everything all right? Please tell me you did not come over just to scandalize the servants."

"No, I… it is better if I show you."

Perhaps Scarlett should have guessed what Tavian meant before he rushed over and swept her into his arms. The kiss that followed was brief, but passionate, taking Scarlett's breath away. More than that, it brought with it

9

images of his memories, exactly the same way that his kiss had let her see so much before. Only this time, it wasn't the long distant past that Scarlett saw.

She found herself standing by Tavian's caravan in the moments after Cruces had whisked her away the night before. How she knew that, Scarlett wasn't entirely sure, but she *did* know it. She could see the almost unnatural good looks of the vampire Rothschild across from her, as well as Tavian's sister Cecilia. Together they looked so similar, with the same dark hair, sharply elegant features and piercing eyes.

She and Tavian were attacking Rothschild in concert. Tavian was lashing out with Cruces' fey spear, which could freeze a vampire in place with a wound, while Cecilia was using a knife that, even if not magical, still looked wickedly sharp. Between the two, Rothschild was having to keep his distance.

Cecilia was talking as she attacked. "You're going to regret using me," she promised, in tones that made Scarlett almost glad that the girl had no reason to hate her too. "First, my brother is going to freeze you, and we'll kill you like the vermin you are. Then, I'm going to make sure that your Order doesn't achieve anything, because I'm going to tell Miss Seely exactly how to find her friend Gordon."

Gordon. Scarlett's longtime friend and fencing teacher, whom she had believed had been helping with the case. It had turned out, however, that Cecilia had been impersonating him using the magic of the fey. The real Gordon had been moved to another world by Rothschild, using one of the magical rings created for the first vampire's "children". The idea had been to force Scarlett into tracking down the magical Devices for him as part of the search for her friend. If Cecilia knew of an easier way to find Gordon…

It was clear though that things were not going to be that simple. Even as Scarlett watched, Rothschild reached out to grab Cecilia, ignoring a thrust of the knife she held and then twisting it from her grip.

"I cannot let you tell her that, Cecilia."

"What are you going to do?" the fey girl demanded. "Strangle me again?"

11

Rothschild laughed. Even though it was just a memory, and even though she knew what he was now, Scarlett could not help being caught up in the beauty of that sound. "I was thinking of something a bit more permanent, this time," the vampire said.

He lifted his left hand, on which his ring glinted golden even in the moonlight. The air next to him and Cecilia seemed almost to split, tearing apart like the seam on a badly sewn garment. Light spilled so bright from beyond the split that Scarlett was blinded for a second. She saw Tavian start forward towards it, knowing already that he did not have the time.

He did not. Rothschild held Cecilia, lifted her, and stepped through the gap he had created as though it were nothing unusual. The gap sealed behind him almost instantly, healing up so that just a second later, it looked like the ragged opening in the air had never been there. Tavian was left simply staring at the empty space where his sister had been.

The vision faded then, leaving Scarlett looking at Tavian from just inches away. She stepped back reluctantly, knowing that even though her parents had little time for the usual formalities and proprieties, they would not like it if someone like Frances were to write to them suggesting that something untoward was going on.

"Where do you think Rothschild took Cecilia?" Scarlett asked.

Tavian shook his head. "I am not sure. It was another world, clearly. Perhaps the world of the fey. It would be an obvious place for them to go, particularly with Rothschild so determined to be rid of Cecilia." His expression grew bleak then. "This is the third time in just days that I seem to have lost her. First when she pretended to go missing. Then, when I thought Rothschild had killed her. Now… now it is hard to know even where to begin looking."

Scarlett reached out to take his hand, ignoring what the servants might think. "We will find her," she promised. "Just allow me a minute or two to get ready."

She headed upstairs, trailing Frances in her wake, and retrieved her Egyptian dagger from her bedside table. Lifting her skirt, she strapped the sheath for it to her thigh.

"Miss Scarlett…" Frances began in a reproving tone.

"Frances, the matter I am about to get involved in may well mean people trying to kill me. Would you rather I went unprotected?"

"But your parents…"

"They gave me the dagger. As for how I have to wear it… well, I admit that it would be a little easier if women didn't have to wear such utterly impractical things, and one day I hope to be able to wear perfectly sensible trousers in the middle of the City…"

"Miss *Scarlett*!"

"…but for now, this is the best I can do. If it makes you feel any better, I am about to pay a visit to an aristocrat in one of the most respectable areas of London. Given the reputation of the aristocrat in question, though, I cannot imagine it is that much of an improvement. Now, would you hand me my coat please?"

Frances did as she was told, thankfully, and Scarlett went back downstairs to meet Tavian.

"Come along then," Scarlett said, offering the young gypsy man her arm. He took it without hesitation.

14

"Where are we going?" he asked.

"Where can we go?" Scarlett countered. "We need to hunt for your sister in another world. That means using a ring like Rothschild's. There might still be two more in existence, but only one of them is in London. We need to talk with its owner."

Tavian did not appear particularly happy at that. "You mean…"

Scarlett smiled. "I mean that we are going to see Cruces, Tavian. Please do try to get along with him this morning. After all, he holds the key to getting Cecilia back."

Chapter 1

Since Cruces' townhouse was not that far, Scarlett and Tavian walked to it rather than summoning a cab. At that time of the morning, with people out on the streets on the way to their various places of work, it was actually quite pleasant.

Scarlett found herself wondering if it would be quite so pleasant when they got there. The previous night, Cruces had whisked her back to his home in a rush to keep her clear of the clutches of the Order. Yet she had not stayed, the way he had clearly wanted. She had gone home. After all, she could not simply spend the night in the house of a man like Cruces. Would he have forgiven that?

There was really only one way to find out, and Scarlett was already on her way to find out. She increased her pace slightly, pushing through the crowds, and it was not long before the two of them arrived in Piccadilly. Scarlett moved up the steps to Cruces' house and rang the doorbell, tapping her foot slightly impatiently as she waited.

The door opened within a few seconds, revealing an elderly man with thinning white hair and an almost beaklike nose, dressed impeccably in the uniform of a butler. He looked at Scarlett with the careful neutrality that was the hallmark of any good butler, then at Tavian with slightly less equanimity.

"Yes?"

Scarlett had not met the man before, but that was mostly because the few times she had been in Cruces' home, the vampire had been with her. She certainly knew that Cruces had servants around. After all, Cecilia had been one of them.

"We need to see Lord Darthmoor urgently," Scarlet said.

"I am afraid that he is not at home to visitors at this hour, Miss."

17

"Well," Scarlett said, "he is just going to have to be. Would you tell him that Miss Seely is here to see him, please?"

"Perhaps if you were to call back in an hour or two…"

"It really cannot wait," Scarlett said. She put a palm out to block the door so that the butler would not have any chance to simply close the door. "And if he hears that you have delayed us in this matter, I cannot imagine that Cruces will be very impressed."

She used the vampire's first name deliberately, hoping that it would make the point that they were not casual callers. Even so, the butler seemed unmoved.

"George, who is it?" Cruces called out. "It is far too early for visitors."

"So I was just explaining to the young lady, sir."

"Young lady?"

Cruces appeared at the door a moment or two later. He wasn't really dressed for visitors. If anything, they seemed to have caught him in the middle of dressing. He had on his pants and a half-way buttoned up shirt, but there was no sign of his cravat, suspenders, or outer garments.

18

Scarlett realized that she should probably look away, but she had never had much time for what she should probably do. Instead, she let her eyes rove over Cruces, taking in the hints of muscle that showed under the shirt, his broad frame filling it out really very nicely.

Cruces smiled in a way that made it clear he knew exactly what Scarlett was looking at. "Scarlett. I trust you had a restful night back in your home."

Of course he would refer to it. Scarlett was not about to be ashamed of it, either, so she nodded. "Very restful, thank you."

"That would probably be thanks to the wards around your house," Tavian said from beside Scarlett.

Scarlett raised an eyebrow. "Wards? There were wards around my house?"

Tavian nodded. "I spotted them when I came over. *Someone* placed basic protective symbols around your home."

"Well," Cruces said, unabashed, "you wouldn't expect me to just leave her alone with the Order sniffing around, would you?"

"No," Tavian admitted, "I suppose not."

Scarlett had not noticed the wards, but presumably, that was because she hadn't seen the outside of her house since she came back to it last night. She had certainly been in too much of a hurry when she left it this morning. Briefly, she found herself torn then between gratitude at the thoughtfulness of the gesture, and the inevitable annoyance that came when Cruces did something without bothering to mention it to her. She pushed both feelings to the back of her mind, however.

"Cruces, we are here on an important matter."

Tavian stepped up to her then, and his arm slid around her. Scarlett saw Cruces' expression flicker, just faintly, at the gesture.

"And what matter might that be?" He asked that just a little too loudly.

"My sister is missing," Tavian said. There wasn't anything in that tone. Perhaps he knew that he couldn't afford to upset Cruces when the vampire offered their best chance of getting Cecilia back.

Cruces sighed. "*Again*? And what valuable item has she taken with her this time?"

20

"It isn't like that," Scarlett said. "May we come in?"

"Yes, yes, of course. Come through to the dining room. George, bring tea for my guests, and my usual drink for me. Have you both eaten?"

Scarlett nodded, but when Tavian shook his head, Cruces ordered the butler to find breakfast for the gypsy fey as well as the drinks. They went through to the dining room to wait for them. It was opulent, decorated in tastes that were elaborate, yet seemed to owe much to the lines of the classical world. That made sense though. Presumably, it reminded Cruces of his youth. He kept his appearance as a handsome young man, although he was so ancient that possibly not even that style was old enough to genuinely reflect his first days as a vampire. There were busts of long dead people around the walls, and paintings that reflected scenes from legends. In the center, there was a long dining table running most of the length of the room, and the three of them crowded at one end of it.

"Now," Cruces demanded, "are you going to tell me what is going on?"

21

Scarlett decided that it would probably be better coming from her. "Rothschild took Cecilia, and she knows where Gordon is, so we need to get her back."

"We?" Cruces asked.

Scarlett nodded. "He almost certainly took her to another world, possibly to keep her out of the way, or possibly just so that he could find a way to kill her and other fey like her using whatever Devices he could find there."

Cruces smiled then. "I was under the impression last night that the idea of other worlds was one that stretched even your willingness to believe."

"Well, I've seen more since then," Scarlett said. "We need you and your ring, Cruces. We need to get to this other place if we're to find Cecilia."

Cruces paused for a moment, in which George came in with breakfast for Tavian, tea for him and Scarlett, and a cup full to the brim with blood for Cruces. Clearly, the butler knew what his employer was.

"George," Cruces said, "my friends here tell me that I must help them to retrieve Tavian's sister Cecilia, you remember Cecilia, from another world, where she is being held captive. What do you think? And none of that 'I couldn't possibly say' stuff."

The butler nodded. "I think, sir, that you probably *do* have to go after her. Even if it is Cecilia."

"Hmph. I suppose so. Plus there is Rothschild to consider. He is probably collecting Devices with which to kill the fey as we speak."

"Possibly, sir. And might I point out that this is the sort of thing you do, sir?"

"That will be all, George." The butler hurried off and Cruces shook his head with a smile that was gently mocking. "Well, there we have it. Even my *butler* seems to think I have to help. Well, hold on a minute."

He hurried off and came back a minute or two later with what looked like a series of maps, which he proceeded to spread out at the far end of the table from Tavian, saying something about not wanting to get grease from the breakfast on them. Scarlett noticed that he had not taken the time to finish dressing, leaving her still with that suggestion of his muscles shifting under his shirt every time he moved. With anyone else, Scarlett might have put that down to the hurry to fetch the map. With Cruces… well, Scarlett would never put something like that down to chance with him.

Scarlett took her tea and went up to that end of the table to study the map. Even at first glance, it looked a little different. The land masses were where they should be, but the political units shown were not the ones she had learned in school. The Empire in particular was considerably smaller than its current extent. She suspected that there was more to it than simply being old, however, because with her talent for seeing the unseen, Scarlett could make out faint lines over the map.

Needing a closer look, Scarlett reached into her purse, drawing out the pair of brass goggles she kept there and putting them on. At once, the magic in them worked to enhance her own natural sight. Making the lines she had seen before stand out and others appear. There were hundreds of them. Thousands.

"Leylines?" she asked.

Cruces nodded. "And it is those that let us open portals. Now, can you pick out the right ones for our needs?"

"I thought you might be able to," Scarlett said.

Cruces shook his head with another of those smiles of his. "Hardly. Though if I could, it would make things simpler, wouldn't it?" He laughed. "Why, I might not even need you."

He reached out over the table then, his hand covering Scarlett's as his voice dropped to a level that Tavian, at the other end of the table and still intent upon his breakfast, would not hear. "I might need you for other things, though. Believe me, your talents aren't the only reason I like having you around."

"You like having me around?" Scarlett teased.

Cruces' expression grew momentarily serious. "You were the one who left last night. I didn't make you go."

"You should have," Scarlett said. "A gentleman would have."

Cruces leaned over to kiss her, sweeping his hands up to her hair as his lips met hers. It was so sudden that Scarlett could hardly breathe, yet it was gentle too. Cruces' lips were like velvet against hers as Scarlett kissed him back eagerly.

25

They pulled apart after a second or two. Tavian apparently had not seen them, either. Scarlett found herself almost tingling with the danger of that.

"It is good to see you safe this morning," Cruces said. "And now, it seems, you are to be back in my arms for another adventure."

Chapter 2

When Scarlett pulled back from Cruces, she took a moment to look over to where Tavian still sat, finishing his breakfast. He obviously hadn't seen them. Something else, however, had obviously caught his eye. He stood, moving to the side of the room where a window opened out onto the front of the house and the street outside. There, he stared for several seconds without speaking.

Intrigued, Scarlett moved over to him, wanting to see what was out there. What she saw there, out on the street before the house, quickly had her staring too. A man and a woman stood together there, and they were about as far from anything that should have been in London as Scarlett could imagine.

Both of them wore garments of golden cloth that looked entirely unsuited to the English weather. For the man, it was a tunic falling to his knees, while for the woman, it was a sleeveless dress that fell in waves around her. Both wore sandals instead of shoes.

The man was powerfully built, with a short, dark beard and curly hair. He was handsome, almost flawless, but he stood in a way that favored one side, and as he took a slight step towards the house, Scarlett saw that he walked with a limp. It did little to distract from the sense of power he radiated, though; one that almost had Scarlett taking a step back to match his step forward.

If the man was handsome, the woman was beautiful in a way Scarlett would not have believed possible. Her hair matched the gold of her dress, and fell loosely down to her waist. She was almost as tall as the man, with a figure that made even Scarlett feel a brief stab of envy, and features that instantly made her think of the kind of beauty found in classical sculptures. In fact, Scarlett briefly looked around, sure that one of the busts that decorated the dining room looked like her.

People should have been staring, if not at the sheer beauty of the woman, then certainly at the way the two were dressed. They were dressed like something from myth, and certainly not in a way that would have been considered normal in London, yet nobody so much as glanced at them. That told Scarlett as clearly as anything that they were supernatural in some way, visible to her only thanks to her talent for seeing the unseen. Yet what were they? Scarlett had seen so many things over the years. She had seen the spirits of the dead and creatures out of stories, vampires and fey, the *ka* of Egypt and stranger things. Yet she had never seen anything quite like the two figures standing in the street.

Cruces joined them at the window and Scarlett heard him groan. "Oh, for pity's sake," the vampire said, "what are those two doing here now? Of all the things that could show up at my gate..."

"Are they a threat?" Scarlett asked. "Do you know them?"

"Oh, I know them, all right," Cruces said. "As for whether they're a threat, the answer to that probably

29

depends on what they want. You know, we could really do without this right now."

"So who and what are they?" Scarlett asked.

"Let's start with the what, shall we?" Cruces said. "They are immortals, and powerful ones. The Ancient Greeks worshiped them as deities. The woman is Aphrodite, the goddess of love."

Scarlett could believe that easily enough. "She is certainly very beautiful."

Cruces frowned slightly at that. "Yes, she is. Unfortunately, she is also very determined. Quite annoyingly so. She has a hard time believing that any man could say no to her."

Scarlett saw Tavian look over at the vampire. "You and her?" the fey man asked.

Cruces shook his head. "Not for want of trying on her part, I should add. She took it into her head that a royal vampire would be just the thing to add to her list of lovers and… well, things got a little embarrassing after that."

"I'm surprised that a man with your reputation said no," Tavian observed.

"Yes, well, you don't know everything about me."

Scarlett couldn't help smiling a little at Cruces' apparent discomfort. After all, the vampire spent so much of his time enjoying the discomfort he caused when he punctured social niceties. Still, she eventually decided to let him off. "If that's Aphrodite, then the man with her must be her husband Hephaestus."

"Yes," Cruces agreed, "that's Hephaestus."

"Though I thought," Scarlett continued, "that Hephaestus was supposed to be ugly."

"Don't believe everything you read in the Greek myths," Cruces said. "That particular one is just because of his limp. The Greeks had an obsession with physical perfection. The wealthy would spend their days at the gymnasia, working on their appearance. As a result, they regarded anything like Hephaestus' foot as ugly. Frankly though, we have better things to worry about than whether you find Ancient Greek immortals attractive, Scarlett."

"I didn't say that," Scarlett countered. She blushed hotly even though she knew Cruces was simply making fun of her. "And he's here with his *wife*, Cruces."

31

"That probably wouldn't stop Aphrodite if she were in the right mood," Cruces said. "Though I'm not so sure about Hephaestus. What worries me most is that they are here together. One thing you *can* believe from the legends is that they generally spend as little time as possible with one another. No, scratch that. What worries me most is that they are here, together, in London, on my doorstep, and they obviously want something."

"What though?" Tavian asked, still apparently unable to take his eyes from the sight of them. "What would they want here?"

Cruces shrugged. "Well, assuming that this isn't a social call, just dropping round to see their old friend Cruces and so forth, then it's quite hard to say. They are powerful immortals, a good step up in power from both vampires and the fey. Take our little problem today. They do not need additional assistance to travel between worlds. They can simply do it. They have powers beyond anything I could dream of. People did not worship them as gods without a good reason."

"So there's nothing they would need you for," Scarlett said.

"Exactly." Cruces stepped back from the window. "I suppose that if they wanted to get involved in human affairs, they might need to appoint a champion. Their laws do say that they are not allowed to intervene directly in that kind of thing."

"So it's like the *Illiad* and the older myths," Scarlett said. "In those, the gods were always inspiring heroes to do things, but they never went out and did them for them."

Cruces nodded. "To be honest, I think they quite enjoy it. It's almost a game to them most of the time. Of course, since their laws specify a human champion for human issues, there is one painfully obvious difficulty with the explanation."

"You aren't human," Tavian supplied.

"I wouldn't sound so smug about it," Cruces pointed out. "You aren't human either. Which just leaves…"

Almost as one, Tavian and Cruces turned to face Scarlett.

"Me?" She shook her head quickly. "You can't mean me. What would two Greek gods want with me?"

33

"I don't propose you hang around to find out," Cruces suggested. "If you're quick, you can be out of the back door to the house before they realize that you have gone. It's the one advantage with these greater immortals. They know a great deal, certainly, but they aren't quite as omniscient as they would sometimes like people to believe."

Scarlett raised an eyebrow at that. "You make it sound like it's a bad thing that they might have come here for me."

"I just think that perhaps you have enough to deal with right now without throwing those two into the mix," Cruces said. "Perhaps if Aphrodite were here on her own it wouldn't be so bad. She would probably just want you to get two lovers together or something equally simple. With both of them here, though, I can't think of anything that they might both want that isn't going to be both complicated and dangerous."

"Well, what could that be?" Tavian asked. "We've already established that there isn't much you could do for them, so what could Scarlett do for them that no one else could?"

Cruces shrugged again. "It's hard to be sure. Remember that I haven't seen the two of them in a long time. And it's hard to tell with immortals like them sometimes. It might be that they want Scarlett for something that only she could do, or it might be that they have something anyone could do, but they've chosen Scarlett for other reasons. Really, it could be anything."

Scarlett decided that she'd had enough. She set off into the hallway, with Cruces close behind her.

"What are you doing, Scarlett?" he demanded.

"I'm going to see what they want. It has to be better than standing about in here trying to guess."

"Not necessarily," Cruces warned, putting a restraining hand on Scarlett's shoulder. "Don't make the mistake of assuming that they're nice, Scarlett. Don't misunderstand me, they're not actively evil, but they simply don't see things the way others do. Humans are so short lived and powerless compared to them that they don't see them as important. They don't mean to be cruel, but they *do* love to play tricks, and those tricks can end up having far reaching consequences. Just look at the position Aphrodite and a couple of the others put Paris in."

Scarlett tried not to shudder at that. She knew the story. The whole Trojan War started just because three immortals, one of whom was standing outside, tried to force a young Trojan man to say which was the most beautiful. Even so, she was not going to slip away, the way that Cruces so clearly wanted her to do.

She strode to the door instead, trying to look as confident as she could. It wasn't easy when Cruces was so obviously nervous, hanging back at her shoulder, obviously ready to try to protect her from whatever might be about to happen. Scarlett ignored that and opened the door, ready to call the two gleaming figures over.

It turned out, however, that she did not need to. Aphrodite and Hephaestus were already standing on the doorstep, obviously waiting for her. Up close, Aphrodite was even more lovely. Her eyes seemed to gleam and shift like oyster pearls, while the rose and honeysuckle scent of her drifted in as soon as the door opened. Even Hephaestus was an imposing presence, standing there behind her looking grim.

"Ah, there you are," Aphrodite said. "We were just about to press this curious device for attracting attention." She indicated the doorbell. "Well, Cruces, are you going to invite us in?"

Chapter 3

Cruces stepped forward. Scarlett couldn't help noticing that the movement put him between her and the two Greek immortals. The vampire's broad shoulders meant that Scarlett could not even see around him to them.

That did not stop her from hearing the melodic beauty of Aphrodite's voice, though. The words came to her in English, but Scarlett had the feeling that they were being spoken in another language entirely.

"You are looking well, Cruces," Aphrodite said.

"It has been a long time since we last saw one another," Cruces replied, almost formally.

"Oh, time. What is time when everyone here is immortal?"

"Really?" From where she stood behind him, Scarlett could not see the arching of Cruces' eyebrows, but she knew it would be there. "So you have just dropped in to see how I am? Together? Well, *that* is most kind of you, of course, but…"

"Where is the girl?" Hephaestus demanded. His voice was strong, and again Scarlett had the feeling that what she was hearing wasn't in the same language it had been spoken in, but his voice lacked some of the beauty of Aphrodite's.

Aphrodite sighed, and it seemed that she did even that prettily. "What my *dear* husband means is may we come in? We know that the young lady we seek is in there with you, Cruces. We are not blind."

Scarlett caught the quick glance Cruces gave her, but he did not linger on her. "What is it you want with her?" he asked instead. "There must be a reason, if you are so eager to see her."

"The girl is special," Hephaestus explained. "We know that she has the ability to locate objects of supernatural origin. Even ones belonging to greater immortals like us. From what we hear, she can even handle them without harm. Or is it not true that she possesses the dagger of one of the god-queens of Egypt?"

"Scarlett owns a dagger, yes," Cruces replied.

Aphrodite laughed. "Oh, you are being far too protective here, Cruces. Please, allow us in. What we have to say is not something to be discussed on a doorstep."

Scarlett briefly wondered what would happen if Cruces said no. After all, beings powerful enough to have been worshipped as gods presumably wouldn't be stopped by one vampire. Just that thought was enough to make Scarlett peer out from behind Cruces. She wasn't about to hide behind him if it would get the vampire hurt.

"Ah," Aphrodite said, with a smile that somehow brought to mind images of open meadows and summer days, "there you are. Our Seeker."

That was not a title Scarlett had heard before. "What's that?" she asked.

Aphrodite's smile grew wider. "It seems we have a lot to discuss, doesn't it? Now, if only *someone* would be courteous enough to ask us in. Come along, Cruces darling, you know it's not like you can keep us out."

40

Scarlett heard Cruces sigh. "Oh, very well. Just promise me that you will behave yourself for once, Aphrodite."

Aphrodite raised her hand, looking from Cruces to Hephaestus. "Of course I'll behave. For now, at least."

Cruces stepped back to allow them in, leading the way to the dining room. There, Aphrodite and Hephaestus looked around. While they did so, Tavian moved over to Scarlett.

"Hephaestus and Aphrodite," Scarlett whispered, "I'll explain later."

"There's no need to whisper on our account," Hephaestus said, still examining the room. The god seemed moderately impressed. "You remember the old places, then Cruces?"

"I remember a lot of things," Cruces replied. "But yes, I remember Greece."

"You should," Aphrodite said, looking around at the marble busts lining the walls. "I think I prefer your old residence on Naxos, but at least some of the art here is nice." She smiled at Cruces. "You really must return to the Greek islands some time."

"So that you can enjoy me being chased around by every woman there thanks to your curse, Aphrodite?"

"Oh, that." Aphrodite laughed the bubbling laugh of someone who had just forgotten some minor detail. "Well, you did need to learn a lesson, Cruces. Deciding that you were so irresistible you could say no to me? I simply decided that if you didn't want one of the things I had to offer, you should have the others. Was it so very difficult?" She laughed again, like a naughty schoolgirl being caught out in a prank. "I thought you would *like* having women throwing themselves at you."

Hephaestus looked over at his wife, before laughing and clapping Cruces on the back. "You're the vampire who was able to resist her charms? I heard the story, but I hadn't assumed it would be you. It seems you have more to you than I thought, Cruces."

More to him than Scarlett had thought, too. She was under no illusions about Cruces' reputation, and most of her time around the vampire had told her that it was well deserved. Yet he had somehow managed to turn down the

Greek goddess of love. Not to mention, from the sounds of it, running away from Greece to avoid all the women who wanted him. That was not something the Cruces she thought she knew would have done.

Hephaestus laughed again. It was a booming, hearty laugh, at odds with that of his wife. "Well then, vampire, can we talk to the girl yet? It is you we should talk to, isn't it? After all, it is not your mark I sense on her."

"The mark is my brother Rothschild's," Cruces explained. "It surrounds that of the Order."

"The Order?" Hephaestus looked momentarily surprised. "It seems that your girl has been leading an eventful life."

"I am here, you know," Scarlett said.

Aphrodite looked over to her sharply. "Yes, you are. That's easy enough to tell. And I sense something else." She darted over to Scarlett's side and took hold of her wrist in a grip that did not allow Scarlett any choice as Aphrodite turned it over to look at the inside of it. "There is the ghost of a mark here, Cruces. It did not last, but it was there. Your mark. Protection. Possession." Aphrodite raised an eyebrow pointedly. "Desire. I might find myself jealous, darling vampire. Loving a mortal woman rather than me?"

"Um… you do realize that your husband is right behind you?" Scarlett said to Aphrodite, trying not to blush at the thought that everyone in the room knew what lay between her and Cruces.

Aphrodite let her wrist fall and then waved a hand dismissively. "Oh, Hephaestus knows how things are. How long has it been since we have been together, dear?"

"A while," the god said. He did not sound particularly happy about it, but he did not seem inclined to do anything to try to stop Aphrodite either.

"Now," Aphrodite continued, staring at Cruces, "answer the question."

"I don't believe you asked a question," Cruces pointed out. "Do you really wish to do this, Aphrodite?"

"Yes. Now, do you find *her* more desirable than *me*?"

Cruces stepped up to Scarlett then, putting an arm around her. It seemed to be half in protection, and half as a way of making it clear what he felt. Though right then, with the possibility of making a Greek goddess jealous in the

44

offing, the two points seemed to be at odds. "Scarlett is special. She is very desirable, but it does not have to do with looks alone, Aphrodite. You above all others should know that. There is something about her that stirs the heart."

"And more." That came from Tavian. He did not put an arm around Scarlett, but he did step close to her on the other side from Cruces. There was a sense of defiance about the way he stood that made it clear he was not going to allow anything to happen to Scarlett. Though what exactly he could do in the face of such a powerful immortal as Aphrodite, Scarlett did not know.

"Well, what have we here?" Aphrodite asked, looking Tavian up and down. She gave him an almost hungry look, but there was a slight turn to her smile that suggested she had mischief in mind too. "Do you have a name, sweet boy?"

"Tavian." Tavian did not move back under the scrutiny of her gaze.

"A lovely name," Aphrodite said. "But then, you are a most lovely young man. And fey too. What more could a girl ask for?" Her eyes shifted to Scarlett. "What more *could* a girl ask for, Scarlett? A vampire and one of the fey? Have you tried them yet? No, of course you haven't."

"That," Scarlett said firmly, "is none of your business."

"Careful," Aphrodite warned. She stepped forward and ran her finger down from the center of Scarlett's forehead to the tip of her nose. "I decide where to put my nose, and those who say otherwise... well, two young men in love with the same woman is always interesting, but I could make it a lot *more* interesting if I wanted, dear." She smiled wickedly. "Just look at what happened to poor Helen."

"You know, I'm sure you promised to behave," Cruces said.

"Oh, *promises*." Aphrodite shook her head. "It's not like I'm one of the faery folk, you know. Besides, I'm not the one who has offered an insult here."

Scarlett looked around. "Then who has?" she asked. "Look, you can't possibly be jealous of me. I'm just mortal, while you… you're more beautiful than anyone I've ever seen. So what if Cruces likes me?"

"And Tavian," Aphrodite pointed out, not entirely sweetly. "Don't forget your faery boy."

Scarlett managed to keep some measure of composure, just about. She did *not* like having her life discussed like this. "Even then, it's two young men. You're… well, *you*. You could have any man you wanted."

Aphrodite shook her head. "But we've already established that isn't true, haven't we? Though possibly…"

Thankfully, Hephaestus stepped in at that moment, putting a hand on his wife's shoulder. "Behave yourself, Aphrodite, the way you said you would. Remember that we are here because we want the Seeker's help, not because we want to cause trouble."

"I find that there is generally room for both in most…"

"Aphrodite."

"Oh, very well." She looked at Scarlett. "We require your assistance, mortal, in a matter we are forbidden to act in directly."

47

"Cruces said something about that," Scarlett said. "About you using mortals, I mean. But what could I possibly do for you? What is there that needs me?"

Hephaestus and Aphrodite looked at one another, then at Scarlett. It was Hephaestus who finally spoke. "We need your help in recovering an item, young human. One that you will be able to sense and touch where other mortals might not."

"All right," Scarlett said. It occurred to her that the best way to go about it was probably just to treat it the way she would any case. "So what is the item?"

Aphrodite and Hephaestus spoke together. "Cupid's bow."

Chapter 4

Scarlett stared at the two immortals for several seconds, trying to work out if they were serious, and then trying to recover from her shock when she decided that they probably were. *Treat it like a normal case*, she reminded herself, though that was far from easy. Normal cases did not involve figures out of myth. This was far stranger than any of the ghosts or other creatures Scarlett normally saw.

"Why would you need my help in helping you find Cupid's bow?" she asked. "Surely, you could find it much more easily than I could?"

"It is a little more complicated than that," Hephaestus said.

"A lot more complicated," Aphrodite corrected, smoothing out the folds of her dress in what seemed to be almost a nervous gesture. "Cupid, my son, has never really grown up."

"He has never tried to," Hephaestus said. "He still goes around looking like a young boy even though he is centuries old. He thinks it lets him get away with those tricks he plays."

Scarlett wasn't sure that she wanted to get between two immortals who seemed to be on the verge of an argument, but she needed to know more about what was going on.

"What sort of tricks?" she asked.

"Oh, he likes to shoot that bow of his at people," Aphrodite said, with a smile that seemed more than a little amused with the idea. "And of course, those he hits fall in love. It is the power of the bow. Well, his power, really, but he's so bound up with that bow of his, dear thing."

"He's lucky Zeus didn't strangle him with it, after his latest effort," Hephaestus snapped. "Honestly, I told you that no good would come of letting him go around watching mortal players."

"Really?" Aphrodite said. "Well perhaps if you hadn't been so busy minding that forge of yours…"

"What happened?" Scarlett asked, and for a moment, both immortals glared at her. It was all she could do not to wilt under the combined weight of their gazes. "I need to know so that I can have the best possible chance of finding the bow. Please, just try to tell me everything."

"He saw the plays of one of those modern playwrights," Aphrodite said. "Shake something or other."

"Shakespeare?" Scarlett tried to contain her incredulity. "But he lived three hundred years ago."

"Immortals," Cruces said softly. "The greater ones in particular have little concept of time."

"Now personally," Aphrodite continued, "I don't think that he has anything on Euripides, but Cupid seemed to like him. And… well, one of the plays gave him an idea."

"Which play?"

"*A Midsummer Night's Dream*," Hephaestus supplied.

Scarlett quickly ran through all the possible ideas that play might have given someone like Cupid. There were a lot to choose from.

"What exactly did he do?" Scarlett asked.

"He found a queen of the fey visiting the mortal realm," Aphrodite answered, "and he arranged for a donkey to be nearby. You can presumably guess the rest."

Scarlett could. She wasn't sure that she could guess at the kind of trouble it would cause, though. "What happened to the bow, then?"

"It turned out that the *king* of that particular group of fey was friends with Zeus, our leader," Aphrodite said. "He complained to Zeus quite vociferously, and Zeus told my son that if he could not use his bow responsibly, then he did not deserve to have it."

"So he confiscated it?" Scarlett said. "I'm sorry, but I don't think I'm the right person to just go up to an immortal and ask him for your son's bow back."

Aphrodite sighed. "Don't be foolish. If Zeus had kept the bow, I would have been able to persuade him to hand it back long before now."

"Persuading people always was your strong point," Hephaestus muttered.

"You never complained when it was you I was trying to persuade," Aphrodite shot back.

Scarlett looked from one to the other of them. "So what did happen to the bow?"

"Zeus hid it," Aphrodite said. "He took it from Cupid and he put it somewhere else. He won't say where."

"Our best guess at the moment is that he placed it somewhere in the keeping of the fey, as a way of placating their king," Hephaestus added.

"That is just a guess though," Aphrodite continued. "Really, he could have put it anywhere."

"Even so," Scarlett said, turning the problem over in her mind, "presumably, you are much better placed to find the bow than I am. This is an immortal affair, not a mortal one, and I don't know anything about the lands of the fey. I have only recently discovered that places like that might exist at all."

Aphrodite moved over to one of the busts that lined the room. It was the one that appeared to be of her.

"Believe me, if we could deal with this directly, we would."

"Zeus has declared that immortals such as us may not search for the bow," Hephaestus explained. "I do not believe he wishes to make it impossible to recover, but he does not wish to make it easy, either."

"He probably intends it as a lesson," Aphrodite said with a sigh, "he generally does. Something about how little trouble keeping a more careful watch on my son would have been, compared to this, probably. You know, I don't think this artist has quite captured the curve of my neck correctly."

"Is this really the time for your vanity?" Hephaestus demanded.

Aphrodite smiled back at him. "I find that there should always be time to appreciate beauty. You agree with me, don't you, Scarlett? After all, you have so many young men appreciating you."

Scarlett shook her head. "If you think that is going to make it more likely for me to help you, you are mistaken."

"But you must help," Aphrodite said. "You have the gift as a Seeker."

"Possibly," Scarlett agreed, "but that does not mean I will help you. You have been nothing but insulting since you..." she paused as Cruces put a warning hand on her shoulder. Scarlett let out a breath. She knew the vampire was right. She could not afford to insult Aphrodite. Thankfully, she already had a way out of having to do what the Greek immortal wanted. "I don't have time to take on a search like this," she said. "I am already busy searching for..."

"We know what you are searching for, Scarlett," Hephaestus said. "Or rather whom."

Aphrodite smiled again, without much warmth. "It might even be that our searches might happen to coincide. After all, not long before we departed for this place, we spotted a young fey woman and a rather handsome vampire coming into the immortal realms."

"Rothschild?" Cruces asked.

Aphrodite nodded. "Now that you mention it, it *did* look a lot like him."

"And of course, you did not think to mention this before," Cruces pointed out. Scarlett had to admit she was thinking the same thing. After all, Aphrodite had already commented on Rothschild's mark, and she clearly knew his importance.

Aphrodite shrugged. Beautifully, of course. "Was there a reason to mention him before? Oh, you might also be interested in knowing that a little time before those two showed up, another young man arrived. Young, quite handsome, dressed in the kind of stiff nonsense that passes for clothing these days. I believe you have an interest in him, too."

"Gordon?" Scarlett asked. "You saw Gordon in this realm of yours? He's there?"

"Well, he *was* there," Aphrodite said, obviously happy that she finally had Scarlett's attention. "We had to leave in a hurry to come here and ask you for your help. Ask, you'll note. We have not commanded you, or compelled you, or anything of that kind, when it would have been easy to do."

Hephaestus shook his head. "I do not believe that making threats will help, Aphrodite. The girl is stronger

56

willed than most mortals, and your games will only make things more difficult."

Scarlett had to admit that praise from a Greek god was pleasant, and he was right; her dislike of Aphrodite did make part of her want to tell them no, regardless of the consequences. At the same time though, Scarlett knew that if these two did have information on exactly where Gordon and Cecilia had gone, it was possibly the best way to shorten the searches for them.

Perhaps Aphrodite realized that, because in an instant, her expression became contrite. "This is about the safety of my son. I will do whatever I have to in order to get his bow back."

It wasn't quite an apology, but Scarlett suspected that it was as close to one as she was going to get. She couldn't imagine that immortals who had been worshiped as gods spent much of their time apologizing. Even so, there was one obvious question.

"Why is this about his safety?" Scarlett asked. "It sounds more like Zeus just took a dangerous toy away from him."

"They said before that his power was bound up in the bow," Tavian said. It had been so long since he had last spoken that Scarlett had almost forgotten he was there.

Aphrodite nodded. "Clever as well as handsome. Scarlett here is a lucky girl. Yes, my son's power is bound up with his bow. It makes the thing more powerful, but it is also a weakness. Away from his bow, Cupid is separated from his power. In time, it would fade from him completely, leaving nothing more than a mortal boy."

"An obnoxious ten year old prankster of a mortal boy," Hephaestus added.

Aphrodite glared at him. "A mortal boy nonetheless. Leaving him without his bow would be a death sentence." She looked to Scarlett. "If there were another way to help him, I would take it, but you are our best chance to find the bow."

Scarlett swallowed back any thoughts of a sharp retort. Aphrodite was right. She could help. And leaving an immortal being to become mortal wasn't something she could do with a clear conscience. More than that, in doing so, she stood a chance of finding both Gordon and Cecilia, so the whole trip was in her best interest anyway.

"I think we have to help them," she said to Cruces and Tavian. "Our goals are similar enough, and it's the best way to help the others. Agreed?"

Cruces and Tavian both nodded.

Scarlett looked back at Aphrodite. "So, how are we to get to the immortal world?"

"Zeus has limited our powers," Hephaestus answered. "It is part of the injunction against interfering. We cannot bring mortals back with us, or anything of the mortal realm. His anger over Cupid's latest folly was great."

"But dear Cruces' ring should help you to cross over with ease," Aphrodite said. "Meaning that none of that should be a problem. I assume you still have it, vampire? I remember it being so very useful to you back in the old days."

Cruces nodded, and if he noticed the attempt to remind everyone of the history between the two of them, he did not show it. "Of course. In fact, Scarlett has just proved instrumental in recovering it for me."

Aphrodite looked Scarlett up and down again. "Then perhaps we will see the bow again. I hope so. For one thing, it will mean getting my full powers back. I'm sure the young man here, Tavian is it, would appreciate the opportunity to be taken to the immortal realm by a goddess, rather than having to fool around with Devices."

Scarlett glanced at Tavian then, and she wasn't entirely happy to see that the gypsy fey's eyes were locked onto Aphrodite. Cruces didn't seem entirely happy about it either. Indeed, his expression right then was almost one of anger.

Chapter 5

"The sooner all this is done with, the better," Hephaestus said. "Zeus is watching us carefully so that we do not use our powers, and has threatened to take them away if we do the wrong thing. It is severely limiting how we can act."

"It would be worse if he actually did take them," Aphrodite pointed out. "Bad enough that my son has lost the ability to affect mortals now that he has been stripped of his bow. What would mortals and others do when it came to love without my influence?"

"They'd probably be better off," Cruces muttered under his breath, but not quite quietly enough to keep everybody in the room from hearing. Scarlett had to bite her lip to keep from laughing, while even Hephaestus seemed amused by it.

Aphrodite reddened with anger, though even like that, she somehow managed to be beautiful. "So you think that what I do isn't important?" she demanded.

"I'm sure that's not what Cruces meant," Scarlett interjected. Apparently, it was the wrong thing to do, because Aphrodite turned to her with a thoughtful smile.

"Yes," she said, "that might work. A little lesson for you all in the power of what I do." She pointed at Cruces. "You, vampire, were so eager to reject me before, yet you want her." She pointed at Scarlett. "So let's make that clear. You will love her, with all your heart. Of course, she will now know that it is simply my power at work. And she will have other distractions, because *she* will love... ah yes, the beautiful gypsy boy. Such a sweet boy. I think he deserves your love more than the vampire, don't you, Scarlett?"

Scarlett wanted to answer, but right then, it felt like the room was spinning. She struggled to sit down at the dining table, forcing herself to focus as she looked at first Cruces, and then Tavian. The vampire looked pained, even frightened. So fast that Scarlett could barely keep up with the movement, he rushed over to her, cupping her face in his hands as his eyes bored into hers.

"Please Scarlett, whatever you are feeling, fight it. I need you. I love you. I have spent so long trying to find you. Don't let that go now. Kiss me. Kiss me and know that it's true."

Cruces leaned forward, obviously about to kiss her. For a moment, it seemed like the most obvious thing in the world, except a second later, she felt a tug on her arm, jerking her around to face Tavian. So close to him there was no contest. The vampire was good looking, but he was not the man she loved. He was not the man she needed with every fiber of her being right then. In that moment, Scarlett wanted nothing more than to throw herself at Tavian and kiss him until they were both exhausted from kissing.

The look in Tavian's eyes told her that he felt exactly the same way. There was such love in his expression, such need, that Scarlett knew that they were perfect for one another. How could she have ever felt anything else? How could she have ever felt anything for some vampire when Tavian was there, and they both loved one another so much?

"Scarlett!" Cruces cried out, and the word was enough to get Scarlett to look back at him. What did the vampire want? Could he not see that she was busy with the man she loved? "God I wish I had told you everything about me and you before Aphrodite showed up with this crazy spell. If I had, you would know the Seeker and the Keeper are meant to be together, always forever. You and I. Not you and anyone else."

Scarlett shook her head. It wasn't like that. It couldn't be like that. It was Tavian she was meant to be with. Tavian she wanted to kiss, and so much more, right there and then.

Aphrodite's laugh cut through the room. "You've left it a little late for that, Cruces. Can't you see that your Scarlett, the Seeker you have sought for eternity, is giving the gypsy boy the look of a woman who wants more than a sweet chaste kiss? I can practically taste the heat between them. Mmm… this should be fun."

Scarlett found herself wanting to agree. It would be fun, if only all these people would go away and leave her alone with Tavian. Cruces didn't seem to agree though. If anything, he looked ready to strike the Greek goddess. Scarlett did not want that, if only because the fight that would surely follow might injure Tavian. Thankfully though, the vampire seemed content to merely grit his teeth and clench his fists.

"What will it take for you to undo this?" he demanded.

"Why would I want to do that?" Aphrodite asked.

"I don't want you to do it," Scarlett pointed out.

Aphrodite smiled. "I know you don't, dear. Come on, Cruces. Tell me why I should?"

Cruces pointed at Scarlett. "Perhaps because in her present state, Scarlett is going to be too busy kissing Tavian to bother retrieving Cupid's bow? She certainly won't get through the portal without my help."

Aphrodite's eyes narrowed at that. "You're threatening my son?"

"I am making a proposition," Cruces countered. "I will take Scarlett through the portal to retrieve the bow, and in return, you will undo what you have done to her, leaving her free to fall in love with me as she should have done before."

"Please don't," Scarlett begged, moving to wrap her arms around Tavian. Aphrodite snapped her fingers, and although Scarlett found that she still loved the gypsy boy more than anything, she did not have quite the same urge to throw herself at him there and then.

"Just a little toning down," Aphrodite said, "so that we can talk without anybody ripping off anyone else's clothes. We wouldn't want a repeat of Thebes, after all." She looked over to her husband. Hephaestus nodded gravely, and Aphrodite pouted. "Oh, very well. You are to take Scarlett through to the immortal realm, assist her in finding the bow, and get it back to me safely. If you do that, I will remove my compulsion from the girl. Of course, who she falls for after that is her own affair. I make no promises."

"Done," Cruces said eagerly. "As long as I have a fair chance to win her over, it is enough. I know that with that, things will turn out as they should."

"I wouldn't be so confident, if I were you," Aphrodite countered, "but that is none of my concern, so long as you retrieve the bow. It will be as you ask. Now, shouldn't you be going? Your Seeker will tell you where to go through, of course."

"Of course," Cruces said. He turned to Scarlett, pulling her away from Tavian through simple strength. It was all Scarlett could do not to lash out at him. Tavian was less restrained. He yanked Scarlett back towards him, almost pulling her away from Cruces.

"What do you think you're doing?" Tavian demanded.

"I'm getting ready to leave," Cruces replied. "Scarlett and I need to be in physical contact when I use the ring to transport us."

"And me," Tavian said. "You are not leaving me behind."

"I think you'll find that I am," Cruces said. "For one thing, there are the effects of this love spell to consider."

"I am going where Scarlett goes," Tavian snapped back. "She promised to find Cecilia with me before she agreed to find this bow."

"I did," Scarlett agreed, turning to kiss Tavian soundly on the lips. It was a pleasant kiss, and she was just starting to enjoy it even more when Cruces pulled her away from Tavian.

"I thought you toned the effect down?" the vampire demanded of Aphrodite.

"A little," the Greek goddess replied, "but only a little. It wouldn't be any fun otherwise."

"Well then, Tavian will have to stay behind," Cruces said.

Scarlett shook her head firmly. "No. He is coming with us. I am the one who is meant to find this bow, so I decide. I want Tavian with us. I love him, Cruces. I... I'm not going if you won't allow it. I don't think I could be apart from him like that."

"Scarlett," Cruces said softly.

"Cruces." Scarlett tried to be firm. She could see that Cruces was obviously struggling against something standing there, but that was just the natural possessiveness of a vampire, wasn't it? Scarlett was not going to allow herself to be parted from Tavian simply because Cruces thought he should be able to sink his fangs into her.

68

"You are as lovely as any goddess," Cruces whispered to her.

"I really do not think that is appropriate," Scarlett replied. "Not now that I have…"

Cruces raised a hand. "All right. Please do not say it."

"Tavian can come with us?" Scarlett asked. She wanted to be certain on that point. Part of her knew exactly what Aphrodite had done to her, but that did not make the thought of leaving him behind any less painful.

Cruces hesitated for a moment, and then nodded sharply. "If he must."

Tavian looked at him then, and patted the vampire's shoulder in a brotherly fashion. "So where to?"

"That is for Scarlett to determine," Cruces said. "Scarlett? What comes to mind? How will we find Cupid's bow?"

"Cecilia and Gordon, too," Scarlett said.

"Yes, of course, Cecilia and Gordon, too," Tavian said.

For a moment, Scarlett did not know. She was not sure quite what it was she was meant to do. Then Aphrodite and Hephaestus walked over to her, placing their hands on her. Their touch was almost electric, and as it came, images came with it. They swam across her vision one by one. Images of a place where the skies were blue, where waves pounded against sandy beaches, and where buildings that were in an ancient style, but which still looked new and cared for stood.

"It looks like Athens," Scarlett said, thinking back to some of her parents' archaeological journeys overseas, "only it is different. It looks... almost like Athens would have been centuries ago. There are buildings where the ruins would be, and they have the same kind of columns, but they aren't collapsing. It's like they are brand new."

Cruces nodded. "I know the place that you mean. It will not take much to get us there."

He reached out to put a hand on Scarlett's shoulder, and Scarlett saw him reach down for the ring that he wore with no warning. Did he intend to leave Tavian behind? Scarlett was not about to allow that to happen. She turned, trying to shout a warning to the gypsy boy, but it appeared that it was unnecessary. Tavian's hand clamped onto her wrist in the instant before Cruces did something with his ring that Scarlett could not see.

The instant after that, the world around them changed.

Chapter 6

For several moments after Cruces did whatever it was he had done to the ring he wore, Scarlett felt like the universe was spinning around her. It was a strange feeling, both terrifying and curiously exhilarating at once, as if Scarlett was, for that moment, the focal point of everything around her. To step between worlds like this made her feel almost invincible, since she was doing something most girls simply could not dream of, and yet also curiously vulnerable. For the few moments while they were between worlds, it felt like the simplest things no longer applied. If they could do this, after all, how could any of the basic rules of the universe be real?

Then they arrived at their destination, and Scarlett no longer had time for that kind of thought. She was too busy staring around her. The houses looked… ancient was the wrong word. They were in a style that Scarlett's mind automatically labeled that way, but they all looked new, well-cared for. They were like one of the places her parents studied that had come to life.

It all looked Greek, with the marble buildings and brightly painted statuary of the classical style. Columns rose up to support the roofs of the larger buildings, while the people there were dressed in clothing not a long way from the kind of thing that Aphrodite and Hephaestus had been wearing. They were in the right place then which was good news, but there were subtle differences.

It took Scarlett a moment to latch onto them. There was the way everybody was paying attention to one man on the edge of a crowd, who practically glowed with the supernatural. There was the way what looked very much like a spirit shot past, and people's heads snapped around to watch it. People here were actually paying attention to the supernatural, like it was a part of their lives. That normalcy was far stranger to Scarlett than the supernatural ever was. It was one thing being told that they were going to the

Greece of the immortals, and quite another to actually see it. For a moment she reeled, just trying to take the whole place in.

Cruces grabbed her by the shoulders, jerking her back just as a chariot thundered past, drawn by two white horses. The near miss was enough to jerk Scarlett away from her staring temporarily, and they made their way down the streets of the city they were in.

"This is Athens?" Scarlett asked, wanting to be sure.

"The Athens of this world, yes," Cruces replied. "It is probably easiest to think of it as a mirror of the one that used to exist on your world, rather than as the original."

They started to walk, and quickly found themselves in a bustling marketplace, where vendors sold everything from simple foodstuffs to elaborately dyed cloths. Scarlett's eyes flicked from stand to stand while the owners shouted out to her. One oddity occurred to her: she could understand everything they were saying, as plainly as if they had been speaking English. When she mentioned that to Cruces, the vampire shrugged.

74

"It is a side effect of travelling with the ring. Now, have you seen anything so far that looks like it might be a bow?"

Scarlett almost laughed at that, but she saw that Cruces was serious. "You really think that Zeus would have placed something as powerful as Cupid's bow in a marketplace where anyone could buy it?"

"He's done worse," Cruces said, and for a moment, his expression darkened. "Oh, he's done worse. It would probably amuse him to see some poor mortal finding the bow and trying to handle its powers."

"Even if it did not destroy them," Tavian said, "they would abuse the power. They might do it unwittingly, but they would. The bow is not a tool designed with mortals in mind."

"So Zeus and the others would have a good laugh at someone's expense," Scarlett said. She found herself looking over at Cruces. "Are mortals just playthings to the greater immortals, the way they seem to be so often to vampires?"

Cruces' lips twitched a little then, and Scarlett got the feeling that he wanted to say something clever and witty as a response, but he did not. Instead, he leaned in close to Scarlett, speaking so softly that even she could barely hear the words. "You were never just a plaything to me, Scarlett. Never. And you never will be just that."

Scarlett could practically feel the desire radiating from Cruces as he stared into her eyes. She had never seen his expression that intent on her before, not even on the occasions when he had kissed her. How much did that have to do with Aphrodite's power? How much had those few simple words from the goddess done to make Cruces more passionate, rawer, and less able to control himself?

Scarlett did not know, and more to the point, she did not care. Right then, she simply did not feel what Cruces wanted her to feel towards him. She could remember a time when she had, and it wasn't that long ago, but it was not like that now. Yes, she knew that was because of Aphrodite too, but that did not make what she felt any less intense. She turned to smile at Tavian, slipping her hand into his. Cruces groaned and stepped back, but Scarlett ignored him.

76

She was too busy kissing Tavian by that point, for one thing. Tavian bent his head down and captured her lips with his, holding her there for several seconds where it seemed that the market around them did not exist.

Scarlett was quite surprised when Cruces practically pulled them apart from one another. Tavian, meanwhile, didn't just seem surprised. He was clearly furious.

"How dare you…"

"There's no time for that," Cruces said, though he said it with a smirk that made it clear ending the kiss was an added benefit of whatever he was doing. "Come with me, Scarlett. You too, gypsy boy."

He pulled Scarlett over to a nearby stall, filled with bronze and iron work. Fragments of things that had obviously been found, or repaired, or well used. For a moment or two, Scarlett could not see what Cruces had brought her there for, but then she spotted it. There, in the middle of the stall, was a walking stick of very familiar design.

Gordon's swordstick.

"May I see that stick?" Scarlett asked the vendor, who was a fairly young man with dark curls and a friendly smile.

"Yes," he said, but he said it nervously, his eyes widening slightly. "Of course."

Scarlett tried to understand that nervousness. It occurred to her that perhaps the young man was not used to women asking for things directly. From what Scarlett remembered, the noblewomen of ancient Athens in her own world had mostly been shut away from the outside world. Or maybe it was just the strangeness of the way they were all dressed.

Still, the stallholder recovered well. "Although I wouldn't know why a beautiful girl like you would want an old walking stick."

Scarlett took the stick and checked it over. The iron head of the cane was inscribed with Gordon's initials, while a brief check with her back turned to the stallholder, confirmed to Scarlett that the blade within the cane was intact. It was better for now not to let him see something like that, because as far as she knew it was not an idea the Ancient Greeks had possessed. Even the steel of the blade,

78

rather than their usual iron, would make the stick too special for the man to part with.

"This is Gordon's," Scarlett said to the other two. "He was here."

"But he does not have it any longer," Tavian pointed out.

"No," Scarlett agreed, "and that is not a good sign. I cannot imagine that Gordon would have left the sword behind willingly. Not in a place so different from everywhere he has been."

Tavian nodded his agreement to that, and Scarlett turned back towards the vendor.

"Please, can you tell me where you got this? It is important."

The stallholder shrugged. "From a peddler."

"And where did he get it?" Scarlett asked.

Another shrug. "Are you going to buy the stick?"

Scarlett fumbled with her purse, wondering how she would be able to do that. She had money, certainly, but it was in pounds, shillings and pence rather than drachma and obols. Cruces solved the problem by simply stepping past her to drop a number of coins into the vendor's hand. Scarlett did not know if he had somehow acquired the right kind of money, or if he was just doing something that was far more Cruces, and throwing more than the stick was worth at it in the Empire's coin, on the assumption that it would be accepted.

"Now," Cruces said, "where did the peddler get the stick?"

The vendor shook his head. "You know peddlers like to keep their secrets, or other people will get to the next thing before them."

Scarlett stepped up and touched the hand of the young vendor. She smiled her most engaging smile and looked him in the eyes. "I would very much appreciate you letting me know where you think he found this stick," she said, as sweetly as she could. "It belonged to a dear friend of mine, whom I miss greatly, and I would be very grateful for any news of him."

If the stallholder had been resolute before, it faded quickly then. In fact, he looked very much like he would gladly do anything Scarlett asked.

"The peddler didn't say much, but he mentioned that he found it near both the forest and the sea."

"Thank you," Scarlett said, bringing his hands to her lips.

The young man blushed, and blurted out, "I think he meant the area south of the city."

"Thank you…"

"Caesar."

"Caesar," Scarlett repeated, with a smile that seemed to have the young man blushing. "Now my friends and I must go."

She turned to Tavian, who stood there looking at her with an adoring expression that matched the way she felt about him.

"It seems we have to find an area near both forest and sea," Scarlett said, repeating what Caesar had told her. "After that, we will simply have to search for any sign of Gordon, or what could have happened to him."

Tavian nodded, but he looked a little uncomfortable. "That is quite a broad description," he said, "and it could mean many spots."

"But Ceasar made it sound like the peddler meant somewhere specific, so perhaps it is just a question of local knowledge," Scarlett said.

"What do you think, Cruces?" Tavian asked. "You know this place better than…"

Tavian tailed off as they looked around. Scarlett had expected the vampire to be standing just a little way away, yet now, there seemed to be no sign of him. It was as though Cruces had vanished into thin air.

Chapter 7

Scarlett's first thought on seeing that Cruces had disappeared was that something must have happened to the vampire. That did not make her as frantic as it might have just a day or so before, but it still had her looking around for some sign of him. There was none, however, and that seemed more than a little strange. After all, nothing would have been able to grab Cruces without a fight, and any fight involving a vampire thousands of years old would have been easy to notice given how close she and Tavian had been standing to him.

Which presumably meant Cruces had left voluntarily. Would he have run off in pursuit of some clue or other? He might, but Scarlett suspected it was not that.

After all, he had been quick enough to draw Gordon's sword stick to her attention. No, it was far likelier that the vampire had gone off for some reason of his own, either because he did not want to be around her and Tavian, or for the simpler reason that he needed blood. Yes, that would be just like Cruces. After all, he had abandoned their last investigation to seek out a drink from a public house that catered to his kind, so why not this one? The vampire was insufferable sometimes.

Either way, it seemed foolish of him to go off without telling Scarlett and Tavian where he was going. What were they meant to do in his absence? Merely wait around for the vampire to return? That sounded like the kind of thing Cruces would expect. He would wander back in half an hour, or perhaps an hour, having satiated his hunger without a thought for the way Scarlett and Tavian had been waiting. Well, Scarlett was not going to do that when it seemed that they had an opportunity to find out more about what had happened to Gordon, and thus presumably about Cecilia and Rothschild too.

No, the vampire would simply have to catch up once he was done with whatever he felt was important enough to call him away. Scarlett set off with Tavian in her wake, asking people as she went where she might be able to find a spot near the city where a forest met the sea. Some ignored her, but more were willing to help out. They pointed her south each time, and Scarlett walked on.

Gradually, she began to notice more creatures along the way that were clearly not human. There was a woman singing near a fountain who wore a dress seemingly made out of kelp, and whose skin seemed to glow the deep blue of the ocean. When Scarlett saw the number of men crowding around her, she guessed that the woman had to be a siren.

Above, meanwhile, creatures with the faces and torsos of women, but the claws and wings of great birds landed on the edges of nearby roofs. Scarlett tried not to flinch at the presence of the harpies, but given what she knew of the Greek myths, it was hard not to. There were other creatures too. Some, such as the minotaur who wandered through the crowd, his bull's head apparently unnoticed, were strange, but others looked almost human. The three young women arguing around a poet would have seemed normal if not for the faint glow of immortality they gave off, while the crone who walked up to a house and came out with the spirit of a dead man looked merely like an ordinary old woman until she looked at Scarlett, and Scarlett saw just how ancient the look in her eyes was.

"We should ask some of them about Cecilia, Rothschild, the bow and the rest of it," Tavian suggested. "They will see more than most people."

That was a good idea, and Scarlett kissed him briefly for thinking of it. After that, she looked around for an immortal whom she would not mind asking, finally settling upon a young man playing the lyre, who gave off the same signs of immortality that Aphrodite and Hephaestus had. He was intent upon his tune, which was one of such loveliness Scarlett could barely bring herself to interrupt it. Still, there was too much at stake to wait.

"Excuse me," Scarlett said, "can you help us?"

The young man blinked up at her, apparently surprised to be addressed directly. "Possibly." He stared at Scarlett a little longer. "Interesting. You're mortal? And yet you have the sight?"

"I've always had it," Scarlett said.

"So what is it you wish to know? I must tell you, I will not unravel what the fates have in store." The man smiled sadly. "Even if they would tell me, which they never will."

Scarlett shook her head. "It isn't anything like that," she explained. "We are looking… well, for several things, actually. First, we need to find a spot where the sea meets a forest."

As with all the others, the man pointed to the south of the city. "There is sea on three sides of the city," he said, "but there is only really forest to the south. If you look there, you might find what you are looking for."

"There was also a young woman," Scarlett continued. "She might have been dressed a little like me, so she would have stood out. She would have been travelling with a man, a vampire." Scarlett wasn't sure why she put it that bluntly. Perhaps it was simply because she suspected an immortal would be well placed to spot a vampire, where he might not pay attention to one woman in a strange style of dress.

"I think I saw them earlier, though I could not say which way they went."

"Thank you anyway," Scarlett replied. It was important to remain polite. She knew from the myths she had studied the kinds of fates that could befall those who insulted immortals. She knew it from personal experience too, given what had happened with Aphrodite. Though that seemed less tragic right then, given how much she loved Tavian, and he loved her back.

That was moving away from the point though. There was still more that Scarlett needed to know. "Lastly, we are searching for a bow that has been lost."

The immortal's expression briefly darkened, and it was obvious from it that Scarlett had said the wrong thing. "I know nothing of any bows."

"This one is Cupid's bow," Tavian put in.

"I know nothing of any bows," the young man with the lyre repeated, louder that time. "You should go now, both of you. Go."

Scarlett glanced at Tavian, who nodded, and they both hurried off. Neither of them wanted to risk angering a being who might be dangerously powerful. Instead, Scarlett found another person to ask, going back to the woman by the fountain. She was just as willing as the young man had been to point them in the direction of the forest, but again she shook her head and refused to say anything when Scarlett mentioned that they were looking for the bow.

"They'll not say anything, you know." The old woman who had collected a man's spirit stepped out of a side street, dressed in a collection of dark scraps that made her look a little like a crow. "They are not foolish enough to risk crossing Zeus. They'd risk my touch before they risked that."

"And what about you?" Scarlett asked. "Will you help us with this… Hecate?"

The name was a guess, based on what Scarlett knew of the myths of the ancient world. As the barest trace of a smile crossed the old woman's features, she knew that she had guessed right.

"Why would I help you?" the goddess demanded. "Why would I risk Zeus' wrath?"

"You are afraid?" Tavian asked.

"I am cautious. Besides, this is not a matter for the likes of you."

"So you won't help us?" Scarlett asked.

Hecate smiled. "I did not say that. I'll tell you everything you want to know. All one of you has to do is take my hand."

Scarlett shook her head. She knew from the myths she had studied that Hecate's touch meant death. "We will find out what we need to know another way."

"Maybe," Hecate replied. "Though you'll have to be more careful than you are being. Look."

Scarlett followed the line of Hecate's gaze to where the harpies sat on a nearby roof. They were staring down at Scarlett intently.

Hecate laughed. "It seems not all of us like nosy girls asking too many questions. Or maybe they just want to see what will happen next."

"What *will* happen next?" Scarlett asked.

"Trouble, of course." The goddess seemed to take a malicious delight in that. "Trouble for you. Trouble for whoever sent you. It will be most entertaining to watch.

Now go. I have work to do. A pity really. I would have liked to see what is going to happen to you."

Scarlett glanced at Tavian and they hurried off, getting away from the goddess as quickly as they could. Scarlett couldn't help noticing as she glanced back that the harpies had followed, landing on the next roof along. What would ordinary people, without her talent for spotting the unseen, see there? Would they just look like a flock of large birds to them, or would they not see anything at all?

Scarlett tried to ignore them. Instead, she went up to the next immortal she saw, a woman with the lower body of a snake, and asked her the same questions she had asked the others before her. Again, the merest mention of the bow had the woman telling them to go, to get away from her.

And when they went, she followed, the same way that the harpies did. That was worrying, particularly when other non-human creatures started to join them. The minotaur Scarlett had spotted before paced along one side of the street behind them, while a couple of goat-legged satyrs fell into step after Scarlett and Tavian passed the doorway in which they were gambling with dice. A woman

91

who was veiled, and whose hair was a writhing mass of snakes, slipped out from a house to join them.

Previously, Scarlett had rarely found herself frightened by the things that she saw. The things that she saw were simply natural to her, as much a part of the world as people or animals were. With those things though, there was rarely any sense that they meant Scarlett harm, or even that they had any interest in her at all. Here, the feeling she got was very different indeed. As the immortal creatures followed just a little way behind her, Scarlett couldn't help but feel a mounting sense of dread at their presence. What were they there for? What were they planning to do?

Scarlett did not plan on standing around to find out. Taking Tavian by the hand, she broke into a run, darting down a side street and pushing past people. She glanced back, and saw that the creatures behind her were keeping pace, but that only spurred Scarlett on to run quicker. It was obvious now that the creatures wanted something from her, perhaps even wanted to harm her. Scarlett was not going to give them the chance.

With Tavian in tow, and with a host of creatures behind her all the while, Scarlett ran on.

Chapter 8

Scarlett and Tavian ran as quickly as they could, dodging past people and hoping to leave behind the collection of immortal creatures following them. Scarlett still wasn't entirely sure why they were giving chase, but it wasn't like she was really in a position to stop and ask. Besides, she had already found out with Aphrodite how easily the smallest things could spark anger in immortals.

Were they all like that, Scarlett briefly wondered as she ran. Was there something about immortality that meant creatures had to have no patience, no kindness? Aphrodite had been petty with her curse, even if it did not feel like one when Scarlett was near Tavian. Zeus, in turn, had been cruel in hiding Cupid's bow. Cupid was *famously* malicious, and the trick that had started all this had been far

93

from kind. The cluster of immortals following Scarlett, meanwhile, clearly intended nothing good if it should catch her.

And then there was Cruces. The vampire was manipulative, dangerous, and clearly not interested in what others thought. After all, he had wandered off in the middle of their search for no good reason Scarlett could see. Was that lack of consideration a side effect of living so long, or was it simply the way Cruces was? Scarlett did not know. She was not even sure that she wanted to know.

All she wanted right then was to get away from the creatures chasing her. Keeping a firm grip on Tavian so that they would not be separated, Scarlett darted past a woman carrying a large jar of oil, sidestepped around a couple of older men arguing about philosophy in the street, and sprinted along a narrow alley.

None of it was enough to rid them of the immortals. The harpies flew overhead, calling out Scarlett's location. The land bound immortals simply ran, keeping pace with Scarlett. They did not catch up with her, but they did not fall back either. Scarlett found herself thinking of the way a pack of dogs might wear down its quarry before closing for the kill, and just that thought was enough to send a fresh burst of energy to her legs.

In an effort to shake off the immortals, Scarlett decided to try more extreme measures. Some of the houses around her had staircases, leading up to flat roofs, so Scarlett climbed the next one she came to with Tavian in tow, then ran along the edge of the roof until she came to the next house. The gap between the two was small enough that even in a dress Scarlett could leap it, and Tavian followed her easily.

The next jump was not so simple, and Scarlett found her feet catching in the hem of her dress. Tavian's hand snaked out to wrap around her wrist, pulling her up on the other side. Scarlett risked a glance behind her. There were a few immortals following over the rooftops, and the harpies were still wheeling above them in the sky, but most of them seemed to be trying to keep up at street level.

It was time to change tactics again then. Scarlett ran to the edge of the house she currently stood on, looking down until she spotted the taut fabric roof of a vendor's stall beneath. Quickly, so that she could not lose the courage for it, she dropped, slithering along the fabric of the roof and then rolling to her feet once she reached street level. Tavian skipped to his feet beside her, and they ran again while the street vendor yelled something behind them. They turned the next corner...

...and came face to face with Cruces, fighting for his life.

His opponent was a vampire. The bared fangs and unnatural speed made that much obvious. Yet he had almost nothing in common with Cruces. Cruces was refined, even elegant, whereas this new vampire was a hulking thing, stripped to the waist and covered in swirling tattoos that seemed to Scarlett to be similar to some of the things people decorated their bodies with in the South Sea Islands. At the center of them sat the mark of the Order, almost disguised by the presence of the other tattoos. The creature's muscles seemed almost impossibly large, making Cruces appear smaller, yet it did nothing to slow him down.

Cruces was fighting this new vampire, and from the looks of it, he was losing. His shirt was torn, while there was blood on one side of his face. Even as Scarlett watched, the larger vampire struck Cruces, sending him tumbling, so that he had to scramble like an acrobat for his footing. He lashed out with a foot in the manner of the French savateurs, but it seemed to make no difference.

"We have to help him," Scarlett exclaimed, her earlier thoughts of how thoughtless Cruces had been to go off forgotten. "Quick, Tavian."

Tavian didn't hesitate, leaping forward to make a grab for the vampire attacking Cruces. Briefly, Scarlett felt a twinge of fear at that. What if Tavian was injured? What if something worse happened? Should she really have just sent the young man she loved into such a dangerous situation with the intention of aiding a mere vampire?

Scarlett shook her head. She loved Tavian, but that did not mean Cruces meant nothing. He was their friend, if nothing else, not to mention their only way home given that he was the one who possessed the ring to walk between worlds. They had to save him, even if it meant danger. Though Scarlett still let out a small sound of fear as the huge vampire struck Tavian, knocking him back.

Scarlett rushed in then, determined to help. She drew her dagger, slashing at the creature, forcing it to turn towards her. That gave Cruces the opportunity to leap onto the larger vampire's back, gripping it in a hold that would have immobilized a smaller creature. The big vampire just threw him off as though he weighed nothing.

Tavian came back at it with a series of punches. Each one seemed thunderous, but the vampire merely shrugged them off before driving forward into the young man, smashing him into the nearest wall hard enough for stone dust to rise up as he struck. For a moment, just a moment, that left Scarlett dangerously vulnerable, a mere mortal faced with the full might of the vampire before her.

It seemed to recognize that, grinning in a way that bared its fangs as it tensed to leap at her. Somehow, Scarlett knew that her dagger would not be enough. The thing would trap her arm so easily, and that would leave her helpless before those fangs. What would it feel like as they tore into her? Would she even know it when they ripped out her throat?

Something swooped down, tearing into the vampire. It took Scarlett a moment to recognize the harpy that did it for what it was, but by then, there were already other immortals there. The other harpies swooped at the vampire, rending it with their claws, while young men and women with that faint glow that marked them for what they were struck at it. The vampire tried to fight back, but faced with so many foes, there was little even it could do.

It tried to run instead, turning and trying to leap up to safety on the nearest rooftop. The harpies knocked the back mid leap. Then the minotaur grabbed it, seizing the vampire in a crushing bear hug from behind that left even its great strength useless for the moment.

Scarlett looked around, trying to make sense of the sudden aid from the immortals. She saw Hecate walk into the alley, her expression suggesting that she was faintly amused by the whole thing.

"There you are. Now, what good did you think running away was going to do, girl?"

Scarlett didn't know what to say to that. "You saved my friends and me," she pointed out.

"Oh, we cannot have vampires causing trouble in our home," Hecate said. She walked over to where the minotaur still held the muscular vampire. "Hold him higher, child of the labyrinth, so that I might see him."

Hecate looked at the vampire closely, even going so far as to trace the mark of the Order with her fingers. Scarlett noted that the creature did not die from that touch, but then, in a very real sense, it was dead already.

"I do not know this one," Hecate said. She looked over to where Cruces stood, dusting down his clothes. "That one, yes. I know him and his of old, when he was merely immortal and not one of the blood drinkers. This one, however, is new."

Scarlett struggled to make sense of that. Cruces had been one of the immortals before he was a vampire? The Greek immortals had known him as one of their own? She wanted so badly to know more about that, but she did not get the chance. One of the immortals from before, the woman whose face was covered, and around whose head snakes writhed, had grabbed Scarlett's arm.

"You still have not told us which immortals sent you after Cupid's bow," the woman said. Her voice was surprisingly pleasant. "Why do you want to know about it so badly? Who sent you? Who?"

Scarlett might have answered, but Cruces stepped into the way. "That is not your business, gorgon. Which sister are you, anyway?"

"Why don't you look at my face and find out?" the gorgon countered.

"I could sing to them," a siren suggested. "They would tell us which immortals put them up to this if I sang."

"And what good would that do you?" Cruces demanded.

Hecate smiled a grim smile. "Then we would know who is going to get into trouble for trying to circumvent Zeus' will. It is always amusing to watch when Zeus becomes angry. Of course, he might choose to do something most interesting to the three of you, too. Zeus does love to punish people."

Scarlett wasn't sure what to say to that, but there wasn't a chance to say anything anyway. The large vampire from the Order chose that moment to slam its elbow back into the stomach of the minotaur holding it, then wrenched free of the bull creature's grip. It lunged forward at Scarlett, moving almost too quickly to follow.

Then it stopped, toppling to its knees. Its skin took on a greyish cast, and it opened its mouth as if to scream, but it was too late. In under a second, it was nothing but stone.

"Close your eyes, Scarlett," Cruces said, but Scarlett had already done it, realizing the danger of the gorgon next to her.

"What about Tavian?"

Cruces sighed, his hand clamping on Scarlett's arm. "I have him. Now come on while they're still working out whether it's safe to look or not."

Scarlett did not need telling twice. With Cruces leading her, Scarlett hurried away, hoping that this time they would be able to leave the immortals behind.

Chapter 9

They ran again, but this time it wasn't a blind flight through alleys and across rooftops. This time, Cruces led the way with the surety of someone who knew every inch of the city. They ran swiftly, but without panic, following behind the vampire in the knowledge that he would see them all to safety.

When had she come to trust Cruces like that, Scarlett wondered. Particularly since she knew just how little she really ought to trust a vampire like him, one who clearly had no respect for any of the conventions of society, and who was rumored to treat women as mere playthings. Though he had not with her. In fact, he had specifically sworn that he never would.

There was no time to think about that now, though, so Scarlett simply ran as Cruces led them from the alley, dashing with her and Tavian away from the collected immortals. By the time the sounds of pursuit had started up again, he had taken them down a flight of steps towards what appeared at first glance to be an old cellar, hidden behind a bolted door.

Only once they got past that door, Scarlett found not a cellar, but a tunnel, walled with rough rock and sloping down into the earth. It was dimly lit, but even by that light, she could make out images of creatures carved into the rock. They looked a lot like the ones that had only recently been chasing them. Scarlett had been running fast enough that she had to pause to catch her breath, but even so she wanted to know what was going on.

"What is this place?" she asked, crouching down in the semi darkness of the tunnel so that she could recover a little. Tavian sat beside her, while Cruces remained standing.

"The city has tunnels beneath that are sometimes used for what they call the mysteries," Cruces said. "It is the one place for people to come and actually see the immortal. They are prepared for it, so they do not shut it out in the way that they normally would do."

"So it is a place for the mortal and immortal to meet?" Scarlett asked. "Like the night market back home?"

Cruces nodded with a faint smile. "It seemed nicely ironic for us to use these tunnels to *avoid* meeting a bunch of immortals. Now we just have to stay down here long enough that they all lose interest."

Scarlett couldn't help smiling, especially as she heard the sounds of pursuit go past. Yet there were more things to worry about than even a collection of immortals determined to catch up with them.

"Cruces, that vampire before… he had the mark of the Order tattooed on his skin."

Cruces nodded. "The Order knows that we are here. I sensed the vampire, Brutus, while you were retrieving the walking stick. I thought I could lead him away from you."

"How old was he?" Scarlett asked, remembering back to the fight Cruces had had with the creature. "He seemed so strong, even compared with you."

105

"He was one of the Order's enforcers. Their assassins. He was very old, but more than that, his kind devote their whole beings to violence. He became far stronger and more dangerous than a normal vampire his age should have been."

That made sense. The vampire had seemed utterly inhuman, more animal than a thinking being. Perhaps that would make it stronger. Still, its very presence raised some worrying questions. It seemed too big a coincidence that the Order should have sent a vampire like that after them the moment they tried to follow Rothschild and Cecilia. Scarlett knew she had to ask.

"Do you think that Rothschild sent him?"

"Perhaps," Cruces answered. "That would explain how he was able to show up here. To get here, into ancient immortal Greece, any non-immortal would need a ring like my own." Cruces raised his hand to emphasize the golden ring on his finger. Scarlett could remember Rothschild's identical one all too easily. "Unless our sister Lydia has decided to become involved, or unless one of the other two rings has been recovered, neither of which seems likely,

106

then Rothschild is the most likely way for Brutus to travel here."

"I still don't understand why you felt the need to draw him off, though," Scarlett said. "If you had only said something-"

"Cruces did not want to endanger you," Tavian said. He sounded approving, though Scarlett had a hard time believing that Tavian would ever approve of something Cruces did.

"Why not?" Scarlett demanded. "I can fight. I fought, when we ran into Cruces and this Brutus."

Cruces shook his head. "I did not want to risk it, Scarlett. Particularly since I believe that Brutus was sent across to this world specifically with your death in mind."

"Why would he be sent for that?" Scarlett demanded.

Cruces shrugged. "It surprised me too. I was under the impression that Rothschild needed you alive. That he *wanted* you alive, and planned to take you for his own. Perhaps that is it though, perhaps he decided that if he could not have you, then no one would. It would certainly be a good way to cause me pain."

Scarlett did not know what to say to that. Once again, Cruces was reminding her all too forcefully of how he felt, even though he knew that Scarlett did not feel the same. Could not feel the same.

Tavian spoke up again then. "Perhaps it was not he who sent the assassin. The Order does not just consist of Rothschild, after all."

"That is possible," Cruces said, "though then there is the question of how they would be able to send the assassin over."

"They would find a way," Tavian insisted. "Rothschild is not the only one of them with an interest here. I can think of several others in the Order who would think that if they couldn't have Scarlett, they would be better off killing her."

Scarlett leaned over to kiss Tavian. It was a sweet kiss, and as they broke from it, Scarlett saw Cruces looking away. That did not bother her as much as it might have done, though she knew she still had to ask Tavian the obvious question.

"How do you know who is in the Order, and what they might want?"

Tavian raise his hand to gently stroke Scarlett's cheek. "Unfortunately Scarlett, I know a lot more than I care to about the Order."

"Is that because of Cecilia?" Scarlett asked, thinking of the way Tavian's sister had gotten caught up with them.

"No," Tavian said, looking away, "that is down to me. I knew of the Order before she did. In fact, she only learned of the Order through me. I'm not proud of it, but she made her choice, while I stepped away."

Scarlett involuntarily moved back, away from Tavian, despite Aphrodite's spell on her. Tavian had links to the Order? How could he have? How could he not have said something before? Scarlett found herself looking over at Cruces, expecting to see the vampire looking amused by the revelation, or even reveling in the pain it caused Tavian, yet he just stood there impassively.

Tavian, meanwhile, seemed to be almost frantic to explain. "I didn't know better, when I first learned of the

Order," Tavian said. "I was like Cecilia is now. I thought I could learn more about the fey from them, and I was so caught up in that I did not realize what they were for a time. They seemed so all knowing when it came to worlds beyond the human one, and that seemed so... so incredible to me."

Scarlett forced herself to look at him, trying to disguise the hurt she felt. Tavian lifted her hand to his lips. "Don't be alarmed, Scarlett. I'm not of the Order. I never was. I promise you that."

Scarlett glanced over at Cruces then. She knew she shouldn't. She knew that she ought to simply take the word of her beloved. Yet there was part of her, despite Aphrodite's spell, that wanted Cruces' confirmation.

Cruces' smile was wry, but Scarlett thought she could detect a hint of sympathy there. "If he were from the Order, I would have known it."

"How would you have known?" Scarlett asked. She knew that Cruces had been involved with the Order once, but how could he possibly know now?

It was Cruces' turn to look away then. "Some of us are not as pure and innocent as you would have us be,

Scarlett." He looked at Tavian then, before bringing his gaze back to Scarlett. "In this case though, Tavian is telling the truth. As for me… well, I have lived so long, and seen too much. I have had my dark days. I am a vampire, after all. One of the first. There are reasons why we have been feared through so much of history, and there have been times when I was one of those reasons. Do not ask me for details. I will not share them. Some things are better left unsaid."

He reached out to take Scarlett's hand, drawing her to her feet. Scarlett resisted the urge to shiver at his touch. He was still Cruces, despite what he had just said. He would not hurt her.

"With any luck, our immortal pursuers will be gone by now," Cruces said. "They are dangerous, but they are also easily distracted."

"They are not the only ones," Tavian pointed out. "From what I hear, you still flit through life without ever taking anything seriously."

"I take *some* things very seriously," Cruces shot back. He began to walk quickly, taking Scarlett along the

111

underground passage with him. He walked quickly enough that for a moment or two, Tavian was left behind. That seemed to be exactly Cruces' intention though. "You should know that Aphrodite's spell on me makes no difference to me," he whispered.

"You have managed to shake it off?" Scarlett asked, a tinge of hope in her voice. She had no wish to hurt Cruces with unrequited love, and if he could only get over what the goddess had made him feel for her, that had to be the best solution for all of them. It would certainly make things much simpler.

Sadly Cruces shook his head. "What I mean is that I loved you before that, so what she did makes no difference. With or without Aphrodite's curse, I will love you."

"Please, Cruces," Scarlett begged, "do not continue like this. I cannot respond the way you want. I cannot love you back."

"I know that," Cruces replied, "but I hope to make you see that whatever else is true, you need me near to you. You are the Seeker, and I am the Keeper. We need one another, and whatever you think you feel for the fey boy cannot get in the way of that."

Chapter 10

With the horde of following immortals gone for the time being, they were able to leave the tunnels, and Cruces suggested that they should head for one of his old homes to get their bearings. Scarlett would have preferred to search for the location of the bow directly, but she could see how that search might potentially be a long one, and knew that having a place from which to conduct that search made sense.

As such, Scarlett allowed Cruces to lead her and Tavian out of the main city and over to a spot in the Athenian hills, where a large building of white stone stood. It was built in a roughly square configuration, and Scarlett knew enough about the ruins of Greece to know it would be focused around a single open living area, where the majority of the business of the house, or rather palace, would take place.

Yes, Scarlett decided, it was definitely a palace. The building was too big to think of in any other way, stretching up for three stories above ground level, with stonework and statuary that pointed to a fortune having been spent on its construction. Even the gates leading to the courtyard before the house were higher than two men put together. Even here, it seemed, Cruces' wealth was abundant.

Cruces swung open those gates, and as he did so, Scarlett noticed just how tense he appeared.

"Is something wrong?" she asked.

"Not wrong so much as... difficult," Cruces said. He sighed. "Remember what Aphrodite said before about her previous curse."

Scarlett thought back, and her eyes widened slightly as she thought of the curse that would mean any woman who saw Cruces would want him. "It still applies?"

"Aphrodite said as much herself, if you recall."

115

Beside them, Tavian laughed. "And you're really trying to tell me that you do not love being the object of that much attention, vampire?"

Cruces shook his head. "Not when it ends up like this. I need to warn you, what you see inside might be... difficult."

Scarlett tried to think what that might mean, but whatever her imagination came up with, it wasn't the sight that greeted them as they stepped inside. The palace was full. Full almost to the brim with women. Some were beautiful, while others were plain. Some were dressed in the greatest finery known to Greece, while others wore so little that Scarlett found herself blushing on reflex. Some had jewels in their hair, others flowers, and a few simply had their hair braided into intricate patterns that had clearly taken hours.

They turned almost as one to stare at Cruces as the vampire stepped into the palace. Cruces led Scarlett and Tavian through to the central area of the house, where marble couches surrounded much of the space, the floor and walls were covered in mosaics, and columns surrounded a central square of open space where light streamed in.

There were more women there too, almost uniformly beautiful this time, though dressed in as wide an array of clothes as the ones in the courtyard. As with those, they stared at Cruces as the vampire came in. It was almost frightening to see so many women looking at Cruces with such undisguised desire. Even the vampire seemed uncomfortable with it. A few of the women gave Scarlett hateful looks, but those faded as she reached out to take Tavian's hand. A few even smiled then, obviously glad to see someone who wasn't competing with them for Cruces' attentions.

"I feared this," the vampire said. "The curse has not waned. The women here are all ones who came to my family's house, declaring themselves my beloved."

"But I am!" one woman near the back cried out. Almost at once, there was a cacophony of sound as all the other women there tried to shout her down. Several charged forward. For a moment, Scarlett thought that they might be about to attack, but then one of them, a beautiful woman with flaming red hair and wearing only a brief tunic, kissed Cruces passionately. Tavian laughed at that, the sound carrying through the open living area.

Scarlett found it less amusing as Cruces shoved the woman back, only for another to throw herself at him. And another. The women all seemed to be determined to get to Cruces at once, to kiss him and press close to him. She could admit to herself that, in spite of Aphrodite's spell, the sight of all those women throwing themselves on the vampire was enough to make her feel a small twinge of something. Jealousy?

Cruces was clearly uncomfortable with what was going on too. He did not throw himself into the women's arms the way Scarlett might once have suspected he would have. Instead, he pushed them away, trying to dodge them as they came at him. He was surprisingly gentle about it though, never pushing any of the women so hard that she was hurt by it, and being almost courteous about setting some of them aside.

The trouble was that his courtesy was making it harder and harder to keep clear of the women. Scarlett could imagine what it would be like soon with them grabbing for him, all trying to pull Cruces from the others. Who knew what harm they might do, even to a vampire like him? No, Scarlett had to do something.

So she charged forward, pushing her way through the crowd. She was less restrained than Cruces had been, though even so she was careful not to do any permanent damage to the women. This was not their fault after all. They were simply the victims of one of Aphrodite's curses, as much as Cruces was.

"Step back," Scarlett said. "I don't care how much you all love him, behaving like this will do none of you any good. Step back, I said!"

For a moment, it seemed like she might have gotten through to the women. For that brief, wonderful moment they paused, blinking at her like they hadn't seen her before, even though she had been standing there for several minutes by then. Quickly though, one of the women pointed at her, fury evident on her features.

"This one wants to keep us from our beloved! She wants to keep him for herself!"

Too late, Scarlett saw the danger. "No, I…"

The mob of women surged forward grabbing for Scarlett, each of them looking ready to kill. Even if that were not their intent, Scarlett would not have wanted them to get hold of her. There was far too much chance of being crushed or trampled with so many women crowding around. As it was, they also lashed out with fists or with their nails, forcing Scarlett to duck and dodge,

She quickly learned that the best way to fight in a large crowd was to keep moving, because stopping would have meant one or more of the women finally managing to grab her. Once one got a grip, the rest would soon follow, and Scarlett could not afford that, so she fought and ran almost equally, pushing women away on the move, or tripping them, and occasionally striking them if there seemed to be no other choice. Scarlett hated to do that, but she suspected that she would hate being trampled to death rather more, and so, when she had to, she lashed out.

Cruces and Tavian fought beside her, trying to keep the women back from Scarlett with shoves and occasionally dragging them away bodily when they got too close. For the moment at least, it seemed that the women's attention was so focused on murdering their 'rival' that they had even forgotten about trying to get to Cruces to kiss him.

Scarlett tried to think of something that might solve the problem. The three of them could run, flee the palace entirely and head back to the city, but that would solve nothing. There were no guarantees that the women would not simply follow, while there might still be the immortals waiting to question them on who had sent them back in Athens.

Worse, it would do nothing to help the women in Cruces' home. Despite the fact that they were currently doing their best to tear Scarlett limb from limb, they were merely more victims of Aphrodite's cruel sense of humor. They needed Scarlett's help. Except what help could Scarlett give them? Even if she could find a way to summon Aphrodite, it did not seem likely that the goddess would remove her curse. It might even be that she could not do it. At best, she would demand that Scarlett finish looking for the bow, and these women deserved better than to be forced to wait like that.

Yet who else was there to call on for help? Scarlett might be able to see the supernatural, but that did not mean that there were many powerful supernatural beings she could call on. None, in fact. After all, the only supernatural creature Scarlett had a connection to was Cruces, and he was already busy trying to keep the women off her.

That wasn't entirely true though, was it? There was *one* other figure Scarlett had a connection to, and he was undoubtedly powerful, in his way. Though whether she would somehow be able to contact him consciously, and whether he would come if she did, remain to be seen. Yet what did Scarlett really have to lose, considering what would happen to her if she did nothing?

"Rothschild!" Scarlett shouted it as loudly as she could. She also reached back to touch the mark that sat at the base of her neck. The Order's mark, but also Rothschild's. "Rothschild, come here to me. Please."

That the vampire would be able to come if he wished was not in doubt. He had one of the rings that matched Cruces' one. He could walk between worlds as surely as they had. As surely as the vampire Brutus must have to follow them. The only questions were over whether he had heard, and whether he cared enough about what happened to Scarlett to come.

Scarlett felt the skin on her neck beneath her finger heat up to a point where she had to move her hand away. She groaned with the pain of the sudden burning, while an unseen wind seemed to come from nowhere. Scarlett had been banking on Rothschild having told the truth about the strength of the connection his mark created between them, and it seemed that he had.

He had heard her.

The air in front of Scarlett swirled faster and faster. It was not enough to move people physically, but the women around Scarlett stepped back, leaving a space there that was empty and still in the chaos. Then the air in that space seemed to split, leaving a hole. Scarlett tried to look through it to spot what lay on the other side, but there was no time, and in any case she had to step out of the way of another attacker.

So she did not see where Rothschild came from, but he did come. The vampire stepped out of the hole in the world, looked around himself and laughed.

123

"Ah, Scarlett, there you are."

Chapter 11

Rothschild stood there for a moment or two, still as the women struggled around him, trying to get to Scarlett. He looked faintly amused for a moment, and then snapped his fingers. Instantly, there was a space around him, as women pulled back, apparently unaware that they had done so. They did not leave Tavian or Cruces alone, but Scarlett was able to stand in that space with impunity.

Rothschild loosened his collar slightly and undid a couple of buttons on his jacket, apparently adjusting to the warmer climate. "You called?"

Scarlett couldn't help staring at the vampire for several seconds. His golden hair glinted in the sun, while his features seemed almost perfect for the grandeur of the classical setting. He looked as beautiful as any of the immortals Scarlett had seen. In that moment, she had to fight to keep from moving close to him. That reaction alone was enough to shock Scarlett. How could she react like that, when she loved Tavian thanks to Aphrodite? Was it the mark? Was it simply that the connection it created could not be overridden, even by a greater immortal?

Eventually, Rothschild stepped close to Scarlett, his face just inches from hers. He did not touch her, but he was close enough that he did not need to.

"It seems our relationship is improving, Scarlett. I would not have thought you would have called me of your own free will this early on in our relationship."

"There is no relationship," Scarlett snapped back. Rothschild liked to play games far too much. "The only thing between us is your intrusive mark upon me. That it has come in handy in this case does not change that."

Rothschild's eyes sparkled, and his mouth twisted into a smile. "Really? How disappointing. Still, it is a beginning. Now, what is it you wish of me, dear Scarlett?"

Scarlett took a breath. Was it a good idea to ask anything of a vampire like Rothschild? Perhaps she should have thought of that before she summoned him through his mark. "First, I want you to help stop these women without hurting them. Then, I want Cupid's bow back."

Rothschild raised an eyebrow. "What makes you think I have it?"

"I am the Seeker," Scarlett said. "Finding things is not a problem for me. It would be too much of a coincidence to believe that you are not interested in the bow."

Rothschild seemed amused by that. "So you know what you are in full now. Did Cruces tell you? No, of course he did not. Who then?"

"Aphrodite."

"Ah, Aphrodite," Rothschild said, letting out a brief laugh. "The most charming, alluring female who ever was. Or she would be, except I prefer mine…"

"How do you prefer your women?" Scarlett asked sharply. She could feel the power of Aphrodite's curse as it worked against her natural attraction to Rothschild through the mark. Thoughts of Tavian came to her, and with them, thoughts of his sister. "Do you prefer them easier to control, like Cecilia? Or do you prefer that they aren't fey either?"

"Human," Rothschild said softly. "I have always rather liked humans. Especially beautiful ones, Scarlett."

Scarlett forced herself to ignore that. Forced herself to ignore the way she reacted to it, too. "Where is Cecilia?" she demanded. "Tell me, Rothschild."

"So many demands," Rothschild said, with a glance around to where Tavian and Cruces were still trying to keep back the milling women. That Scarlett was safe in this calm spot seemed to make no difference. "To solve your problems, to give back the bow, and now for Cecilia. I might almost think you weren't interested in me for *me,* dear Scarlett."

"As though I would ever want that."

"Careful," Rothschild warned gently. "You might annoy me if you keep going long enough."

"Annoy you?" Scarlett shook her head in exasperation. "You sent an assassin after me, Rothschild."

Rothschild took a surprised step back. "No, I did not. Why would I? I want you very much alive, Scarlett. Believe me on that."

128

Strangely, Scarlett did, though it was hardly a comforting thought. "Then who?"

"Perhaps you should begin trusting me more and your companions less." He gave Tavian a pointed look.

"No, I don't believe you," Scarlett said.

"Really? Even though he was a trusted member of our Order?"

"He said that he never joined," Scarlett retorted.

Rothschild shrugged. "Then he lied. He may not be in it now, but he was one of us before. He introduced me to Cecilia, you know."

"You're the liar," Scarlett said, but she could not get the venom into the words that she wanted. The truth was that Tavian had admitted making just such an introduction.

"Am I a liar?" Rothschild asked innocently, his lips quirking just slightly. "Where have you been getting all your information about me, about the Order, about Cecilia?"

"Tavian," Scarlett said, knowing that she had no choice. "And Cruces."

"Ah Cruces," Rothschild said. His smile widened. "The founder of our Order. A man who would set something like that up and then abandon it. You should ask him about that, Scarlett. After all, we cannot have you running around with inconstant men. While you're doing that, ask him how an immortal like him got to become a vampire, too. What was the price he had to pay for that? There is always a price for things, you know."

"What are you trying to do?" Scarlett asked. "Put doubt into my head?"

Rothschild actually laughed. "I do not have to. The doubts are there, Scarlett. I am merely drawing attention to them. I am showing you what you know your companions to be."

"I know what *you* are," Scarlett countered. "I saw you attack Cecilia, and I was there in Whitechapel."

"And yet," Rothschild pointed out, "you are the one who called me here. Even knowing what you think you know."

"Because I also know you have Cupid's bow," Scarlett said. She glanced around at the chaos. Women had started trying to kiss Cruces again. "Because I think you might be able to help with this mess."

"You know I have it? Interesting. Well, I will admit that a Device like that would come in handy."

"Exactly," Scarlett said, "so hand it over."

Rothschild shook his head in amusement. "Ah, Scarlett."

"What do you find so funny, Rothschild?"

"Perhaps you are not yet as good at finding things as you think."

Scarlett bristled at that. "I have done well enough tracking down the bow."

"Better than you could possibly think. You are holding it, girl."

Scarlett stood there, dumbfounded, trying to work out what the vampire meant. The only thing she was holding was Gordon's sword stick. Which couldn't possibly be...

Rothschild snatched it from her in a single swift movement. He leaped back through the crowd of women to the doorway, leaving Scarlett stranded in a still empty circle of protection. "It is a difficult choice, isn't it Scarlett? Leave that circle, and they will rip you apart. Don't, and…"

He didn't finish that, but lifted the stick to one side instead, flourishing it. Somewhere in that movement, it ceased to be a stick and became something golden and curved instead. A bow. A beautiful, golden, curved bow with a string that seemed to be made from light. It was magnificent.

"First," Rothschild called out, "because I wouldn't want you to accuse me of never giving you anything, dear Scarlett…"

He pulled back the bow string and an arrow appeared on it. Rothschild lifted the bow and fired it over the crowd of women still pawing at Cruces. The arrow seemed to burst into a shower of golden dust, and where that dust fell, women stopped, looking down at themselves with a mixture of confusion and embarrassment. With no women to fight off, Cruces and Tavian were free to look over to Scarlett, but there were still too many people in the way for them to get to her.

"And now," Rothschild said, "you will remember that I said everything has a price? Well, this is mine for helping you, Scarlett."

He lifted the bow, pointed it at her, and drew back the string. An arrow appeared. Before Scarlett could think to throw herself aside, he shot the arrow, and it flew into her. She looked down. There was no sign of it. Then she looked up again.

Rothschild was... he was everything. He was the most perfect man Scarlett had seen. He was more beautiful than anything she had ever known before, and she knew in that moment that she loved him. She had thought she loved Tavian, but in that instant, what she had felt was gone, replaced by her true love for Rothschild. The vampire beckoned, and she ran to him. Rothschild met her with a passionate kiss, but it wasn't enough for Scarlett. She actually groaned when he pulled back from her.

"Cupid's bow?" Cruces' voice rang out over the sudden silence.

"Of course it is Cupid's bow," Rothschild said, with contempt. Scarlett did not care about that. Her beloved

133

could talk to Cruces any way he wanted. "And the beauty is that Scarlett here did not know that she had found it. I assume that the king of the fey must have transformed the bow and placed it here in the home plane of Aphrodite as a way of spiting her and that son of hers. He always did have a sense of humor."

"How did I not find it?" Scarlett asked, leaning in to kiss Rothschild's neck.

"Oh, but you did find it, darling," Rothschild replied, and just to hear him call her that made Scarlett go weak with desire. "You came here, and you found it. You even found a way to take it. You simply did not know that you had. That is all right though. You have still given me a very powerful artifact."

Scarlett pressed herself closer to Rothschild. Part of her wanted to know what he would do with the bow, but more of her simply wanted to feel him pressed to her. She could trust him, that part argued. He was the man she loved, after all.

She glanced up to see Tavian and Cruces with furious expressions, pushing their way through the crowd of women. Why did they look so angry? Was it because

Scarlett did not love them? Could they not simply be happy for her? No, judging by the speed with which they were coming forward, it seemed that they could not.

"Hold tight, Scarlett," Rothschild murmured, and Scarlett was only too happy to comply, looping her arms around him so that she could feel the muscles of his torso shifting beneath his clothes.

"What now?" she asked.

Rothschild kissed her briefly. "Now, we leave."

The vampire lifted his hand, the ring on it plainly visible. He manipulated it the way Cruces had earlier, and for the second time that day, the world shifted around Scarlett.

Chapter 12

Scarlett clung to Rothschild as they traveled, partly to be as close to the man she loved as possible, and partly because the sheer speed of their travel made the thought of losing her grip a frightening one. While they were between worlds, it was like being inside a tornado, and the forces there threatened to tear Scarlett from him.

"Where are we going?" Scarlett asked.

Rothschild kissed the top of her head gently. "Somewhere we can be alone, but first…"

They appeared briefly in a meadow, and Scarlett wondered why Rothschild would have brought her there. Not that she minded. She would have gone anywhere with the vampire. It simply seemed like a strange choice. She only understood when Cruces and Tavian appeared a hundred or so yards away. They began to sprint towards where Scarlett and Rothschild stood.

"They're following us somehow," Scarlett guessed.

"In the seconds after a ring is used, it isn't hard to trace the ripples it leaves in the space between worlds. It is like following in a boat's wake."

With that, he manipulated the ring again, and they were flying between planes of existence once more. Rothschild made jumps in quick succession, so that for a second or two, he and Scarlett touched down on the top of a mountain, on a tiny sandbank in the middle of an estuary, and in the middle of a formal rose garden. Each time, they flashed away almost as soon as they landed, like a gazelle zigzagging to avoid a lion.

Even so, Scarlett guessed that Rothschild must have some final destination in mind, so she pressed the vampire again, trying to determine where that might be.

"Are you taking us to where Cecilia is?"

It seemed like a logical conclusion, given that the two had last been seen together, but it seemed to be one that annoyed Rothschild. The vampire's eyes narrowed.

"Why did you have to bring her up?" the vampire asked. "Surely you don't care about what happens to her after all she did to betray you?"

"She's Tavian's sister, and I still care for him as a friend. I don't know why... when I'm completely in love with you," Scarlett said. "I'm sorry. I know you should be enough for me. I think it's because I gave my word I would help. That I would find Cecilia."

Rothschild kissed her forehead this time. Oh, how Scarlett wished it were her lips. How had she spent so much of the last few days seeing him as evil when he made her feel like this?

"My sweet kind-hearted Scarlett," Rothschild murmured, as he jumped them to yet another world. "How innocent you are, even though you can lay claim to a knowledge of so much of the world."

"What does that mean?" Scarlett asked, as they paused briefly at the top of what appeared to be a stone tower, with other towers around it. "Is Cecilia..."

"Cecilia is no longer a concern," Rothschild said. "For either of us. She won't come between us, she won't be a menace."

"You didn't kill her, did you? I know it would take a Device, but…" Scarlett tailed off. She loved Rothschild, but she also knew just how dangerous he was. Would it stop her loving him if she knew he had killed Cecilia? No, nothing would stop that. Nothing.

"I did not even harm her," Rothschild promised. Behind them, Cruces and Tavian flashed back into the world. Rothschild jumped himself and Scarlett away again, landing on a patch of open moorland this time. "I simply made a deal with her instead. In exchange for my help in getting to the lands of the fey, she would stop interfering with us. A much easier way to be rid of her."

"What about Gordon?" Scarlett asked. "Where is he?"

"Somewhere safe," Rothschild promised. "Without any magic or abilities, there is no reason for anything to happen to him. He is simply out of the way."

"I thought…I thought you would harm him," Scarlett admitted. She felt ashamed of that instantly, thinking something so awful about Rothschild given all that she felt about him.

139

Rothschild shook his head with a wan smile. "I am not quite so bad as Cruces and Tavian must have made me out to be, dear Scarlett. Once you get to know me better, I hope you will see that. Then, we will not have to worry about anyone coming between us."

Scarlett laughed at that and turned to kiss the vampire passionately. "I already love you more than life itself," she promised. "No one will come between us."

"The way no one could have come between you and Tavian? You and Cruces?"

"Those aren't the same," Scarlett promised, because clearly they were not. Those moments had been mere infatuations compared to this. "I love you. Nothing can change that."

Rothschild shook his head. "If only it were true."

He used his ring to jump them away again as Tavian and Cruces got close, sending them into the space between worlds once more. Scarlett, determined to prove how much she loved him, kissed the vampire deeply yet again.

"You are as exquisite as the treasures you will help me to uncover," Rothschild breathed. "You will help me, won't you Scarlett?"

140

"With anything," Scarlett promised, and in that moment, she meant it.

"I must finish the work of the Order, no matter how hard it is," Rothschild said. They were still between worlds, floating in empty, swirling space. It seemed that Rothschild was holding them there for now. "Cruces knew that once, but he came to love humans too much. He spent his time helping them rather than his own kind. He lost sight of what had to be."

"And what is that?" Scarlett asked.

Rothschild looked like he might actually answer. He looked at her deeply and nodded, as if to himself. He even opened his mouth to answer. At that moment, however, another form struck him from the side, travelling with immense speed. Cruces.

Scarlett barely had time to catch a glimpse of the vampire as he slammed into them. His hair was wild and his expression wilder. He had a grip on Tavian's wrist, and the gypsy fey floated along behind him through the void. All of Cruces' concentration was on Rothschild, however, and the vampires struck one another with hideous force.

So much force, in fact, that Scarlett could not keep her grip on Rothschild. For a moment, she scrambled to try to grab some part of him, but she had left it too late. She started to fall away from him, though in this place concepts like falling had little meaning. A horrifying thought came to her. She had no way to move between worlds. She did not have Rothschild's ring, or even Cruces. If she fell here, she might fall forever, or at least until she starved here in the blank space between existences. And she *was* falling.

"Rothschild!"

The vampire could not come to her aid. He and Cruces were too busy fighting in that empty space. Even as Scarlett watched, Cruces kicked Rothschild back, knocking him even further away from her. Scarlett winced at the thought of such harm to the vampire, and briefly, it was enough to distract her from thoughts of what was happening to her.

Not for long though. What would it be like to drift through that emptiness as hunger and thirst claimed her? What would it be like to have nothing to look at for hours, days? Nothing to touch any of her senses? Would Scarlett go mad before she finally succumbed? Or would

142

Rothschild find a way to save her? Scarlett wanted to believe it. Wanted to believe it so badly. Yet in a place as empty as this, how could anybody be found?

The mark, Scarlett told herself, he has the mark to find me. Yet would even that be enough in a place where distance seemed to have no meaning? Scarlett did not know. She could only shut her eyes and hope.

When a strong hand clamped onto her wrist, Scarlett almost cried out Rothschild's name in relief, but as she opened her eyes, she saw that it was not the vampire. Her rescuer had dark hair instead of blond, and was no more a vampire than she was. Tavian. Tavian had rescued her. The fey hung at full stretch in space, one hand gripping Cruces' wrist while the other clung to Scarlett's. With surprising strength given the way he was spread-eagled in the void, the young fey man pulled Scarlett to him.

Scarlett was only too grateful for that. She was not under Aphrodite's spell any longer, and she loved Rothschild now far more than she had ever loved Tavian, but she still clung to him, wrapping her arms around him and refusing to let go. For all that he could never be to her now, Tavian was still her friend. He had saved her, and Scarlett pressed close to him in the void.

A second later, and they were not in that dark space anymore. They were on a beach instead, and Scarlett recognized the buildings of Athens nearby. Tavian was there, still holding onto her, and for the moment at least, Scarlett was glad of the comfort. Cruces was there too, and if Scarlett was angry with him for striking Rothschild, she was still grateful that he had played his part in getting Scarlett to safety.

Of Rothschild, however, there was no sign.

"Where is he?" Scarlett demanded, breaking free of Tavian's grip. "Where is Rothschild? What did you do with him, Cruces?"

"I did nothing," the vampire countered. "And I imagine Rothschild is perfectly safe wherever he is, more's the pity. With his ring, it would not have been hard for him to leave the void."

"How can you speak about him like that?" Scarlett demanded. "How can you hate him so much when I…"

"When you love him?" Cruces asked.

144

Scarlett nodded, sinking down onto the sand of the beach, facing away from Cruces and Tavian, with her arms hugging her knees. How could she be alone like this? So soon after finding out what she felt for Rothschild? How could Cruces have ruined her happiness like that?

Behind her, Scarlett heard Cruces and Tavian talking softly about her. She gave them no clue that she was listening. It seemed better that way. Besides, separated from the vampire she loved as she was, Scarlett simply did not wish to speak.

"She has been shot with Cupid's bow," Cruces told Tavian. "Which means she now loves Rothschild as surely as she loved you before."

"Is there anything we can do about it?" Tavian asked. How could he ask that? How could he want to destroy Scarlett's happiness?

"Not without the bow, and Rothschild still has that. We are back to the beginning, I think." Cruces paused. "Only now, Scarlett is in love with just about the worst man she could be. Even worse than you."

145

Chapter 13

For a minute or two, Scarlett sat there, the pain of separation from Rothschild so sharp that she could hardly breathe. She needed to be near him so much, yet here she was on this beach with only Cruces and Tavian for company. Why had that happened to her? Why?

Scarlett realized that she knew the answer to that one and stood, turning to confront Cruces. "You did this," she said. "If you hadn't come after us, Rothschild and I might have been happy. If you had not chased us, we would have been together. If you simply hadn't struck him in the void, I wouldn't be stuck on this sand without him."

For a moment, Cruces' eyes flashed. "Well, forgive me for thinking that you were in danger, and that we should not permit one of the most dangerous vampires in existence to be left with both you and the bow."

"It's better than being left with you," Scarlett snapped back. "How could I ever have thought…"

"Scarlett," Tavian said, much more gently than Cruces. He reached out to take her arm at the elbow. "Do you remember being struck by an arrow from Cupid's bow?"

"Well yes, obviously." Scarlett looked at him reprovingly. She wasn't some kind of idiot.

"So you know that the *reason* you are feeling what you are currently feeling is because the bow's powers are affecting you?"

Scarlett wanted to tell him to stop being so stupid, and that of course that wasn't the reason. That she simply loved Rothschild with all her heart. Yet she had more control than that, barely. Scarlett forced herself to nod.

"I know that, but that doesn't change anything. I do love him. I love him so badly that it hurts."

"I know," Tavian said.

"And how could you know how it feels to love someone that much?"

The young man smiled wanly. "I think both Cruces and I know exactly how that feels. The point is that we're still your friends, Scarlett. We still care about you, a great deal. Don't we, Cruces?"

The vampire glared at the other man for a moment, but then nodded. "Yes. Forgive us, Scarlett, we only acted because we believed you to be in danger. I'm sorry if you feel we were wrong."

"Wrong?" Scarlett demanded. "Wrong to separate me from the man I love? Wrong to risk losing me in the void, where not even Rothschild could find me?"

"Well," Tavian said, obviously trying to make peace, "it's done now. You can't get him back for the moment, so why don't we concentrate on the other things we need to do, like finding the bow again?"

Gone? Scarlett almost cried out at the pain of that simple word. Rothschild, lost to her. Except he wasn't, was he? She had brought him to her once, so she could do it again. She reached up to the mark at the back of her neck.

"Scarlett, what are you doing?" Tavian asked.

"I'm bringing him back. Rothschild. Rothschild!"

For an instant, Scarlett got a glimpse of cliffs of dark basalt, with a gaping hole opening out onto the Mediterranean. There were statues of white marble set into the rock, depicting monsters and beasts of all descriptions. Then Cruces grabbed her arm, pulling it down to her side.

"Don't be so stupid," the vampire snapped.

"I am not being stupid," Scarlett countered, trying to tear her hand free. Cruces' grip was like iron. "I am calling back the man I love."

"I don't think he will come," Tavian said softly. "Rothschild will not appear knowing that we are here. Not when he has the bow. He would be too afraid that we would take it from him."

"Then you have to go," Scarlett insisted.

Cruces shook his head, and Scarlett made a face. In that moment, but only in that moment, she hated the vampire for standing between her and Rothschild. Then she thought back to the women at Cruces' home. The ones who had tried to tear her apart. She was becoming like them, and there was nothing she could do to stop it. Scarlett felt

149

tears touch her cheeks. She knew she was under some kind of spell, but she couldn't help loving and wanting Rothschild more than anything at the moment. She couldn't even fight it nor did she want to.

"I don't know what to do," she said.

"Maybe you should help us find him," Cruces shot back, frustrated how Scarlett could now be in love with their mortal enemy. "That way, we can find the bow and undo this mess. Though how exactly we'll find him now…"

"He's in a cave," Scarlett said. "A big cave with statues around the entrance, that you have to approach from the sea. I saw it when I tried to contact Rothschild."

"Then that is where we have to go," Tavian said. "We'll need a boat."

Finding a boat meant going back into the town. Thankfully, the immortals there seemed to have found other things to amuse them since they had last been there, but still, the three of them took precautions. They bought cloaks at the first stand they could find them at and wearing them despite the heat.

Cruces did not know anyone who could lend them a boat, but as he pointed out, so close to the sea, almost everyone would know someone who had one. It was simply a question of finding someone who was willing to do business with them. For Scarlett, the answer to that was obvious. She led the way back through the streets to the stand where they had bought what turned out to be the bow. Caesar was still there.

When Scarlett asked, and Cruces supplied the coins, the dark haired young man was only too happy to admit that his cousin owned a small boat he wouldn't mind them using, though Caesar would have to go along with them to make sure that the boat got back in one piece.

"This might be dangerous," Scarlett warned. She described the place they wanted to get to. "Do you know it?"

Caesar nodded. "Yes, I know it. It is on an island not far from here. Not a good place. If you want to go there, though, I can take you. And I am going."

Scarlett had to admit that his willingness to help was hard to turn down. Caesar was even willing to shut down his stall immediately and accompany them down to the docks, where the boat waited. It wasn't large, and Caesar's cousin probably used it for fishing judging from the smell, but it was big enough for their needs, having both oars and a small mast.

They made good time, out on the open water beyond the docks. Caesar turned out to be a good sailor, piloting the boat with ease. Cruces and Tavian also seemed to know what they were doing, and helped with the sails, so that they drifted along at a good speed with the help of the wind. That was good. The faster they travelled, the faster Scarlett could be back with Rothschild.

They had been travelling for a couple of hours when Scarlett caught sight of the cliffs ahead. They were sharp, jagged things, surrounding an island, and in the middle of them there sat an opening so large that it could have swallowed a much larger boat than theirs. Slowly, they brought the boat closer.

It was then that she heard the singing. The voice was female, and beautiful almost beyond words, but strangely familiar. It seemed to be coming from the rocks away to their left, right where they were sharpest and most dangerous. It was only as Scarlett looked over and saw the kelp clad form of a young woman sitting there that she remembered where she had heard singing like that before. It had been in the Athens market, where a siren had been singing by the fountain.

Scarlett felt the small boat jerk as it heeled around, pointing them straight towards the immortal creature on the rocks. She looked back to see that Caesar's face was enraptured, while nearby, Tavian was removing his shirt, obviously in preparation for throwing himself into the waters around them.

Scarlett acted on instinct, tackling Tavian low around the legs. It was a dangerous move to try on a boat, and Scarlett braced herself for the possibility of hitting the water as they fell, but she had judged it right. They hit the deck together in a bundle, and Tavian pushed at Scarlett, trying to get up.

Cruces, meanwhile, had moved over to Caesar. For one horrible moment, Scarlett thought he might have been caught by the song too, but then the vampire reached out to grab the tiller. The two struggled, and though Cruces

153

clearly had the greater strength, Caesar fought hard, striking at the vampire and trying to knock him away.

Scarlett had her own problems right then, though. Tavian shoved her back, and almost struggled to his feet. Scarlett managed to kick his legs from under him, but Tavian scrambled back up, looking at her furiously. Scarlett reacted in the only way that seemed safe, lashing out with a punch with her whole weight behind it. By luck as much as skill, she caught Tavian sweetly on the jaw, and he collapsed into unconsciousness.

"I'm sorry," she said, stepping past him to help Cruces with Caesar. Between them, they were able to drag the man over to the mast, and then tie him to it with lengths of rope taken from the boat. Caesar fought to get free, but quickly, Scarlett was able to take control of the tiller, steering them away from the rocks while Cruces secured Tavian the same way they had Caesar.

"How were you not affected?" Scarlett asked once they were safe. "I thought a siren's song drove all men mad with desire."

"I am powerful enough to ignore such a creature," Cruces said. "The more interesting question is how you were able to ignore it, Scarlett."

"I am not a man," Scarlett pointed out.

"I had noticed," Cruces replied with a smile, "but that is unlikely to be it. Sirens can affect all mortals. They make them feel that their greatest desire lays their way. It is men you hear about simply because most sailors are men. Yet you were safe."

"Perhaps it is my love for Rothschild," Scarlett suggested. "I love him so much that no magical trickery could make me desire anything else."

Cruces shook his head. "Perhaps, though I doubt it. For now, it is enough that we are safe."

He nodded past Scarlett, to where the siren had been singing. She had stopped now, and stood on the rocks with her hands on her hips. With a gesture of annoyance, the immortal leaped from them out into the sea and disappeared from view.

"It seems we are no longer interesting to her," Scarlett said.

"Or perhaps she simply does not dare follow us into the cave. Now, let us free the other two and bring Tavian around. That was some punch."

"It was what I had to do," Scarlett replied.

"Yes. Sometimes, we must all do things we do not like."

Scarlett was going to ask Cruces what he meant by that, but by then, the vampire was busy freeing the others. Neither man seemed angry at what had needed to be done to them, and their boat quickly resumed its passage towards the mouth of the great cave that dominated the coast of the island. Was Rothschild really in there? Scarlett hoped so.

Chapter 14

Closer to the cave, Scarlett could see the marble statues around it. They were sunk into niches in the rock, so that the contrast between the white of the marble and the black of the basalt was striking. Now that she was seeing them in life and not through a vision, Scarlett could make out their details as the small boat they occupied, bobbed closer.

Those details were not pleasant. The statues were not the ones to be found back in town or in Cruces' home. Those were grand, painted statues of men and women, gods and other immortals, who were invariably as beautiful as the sculptor's art could make them. These were different. They were well sculpted, but they were not beautiful, because the things they showed could never be anything other than terrifying. There were great beasts and monsters seemingly composed of several animals put together, things out of legend and things out of nightmare.

Scarlett mentally checked them off one by one as she identified them, picking out the griffon, the hippogriff, the manticore. There were a few that she could not identify though, stranger things that had no names in the legends Scarlett studied. Above them all, at the apex of the cave opening, sat a statue that was long and sinuous in design. It depicted a serpent, coiling around what appeared to be a boat in the same style as the one they were currently travelling in. It was enough to make Scarlett shudder.

Mere statues were not going to stop her from getting to Rothschild though, assuming that he was indeed in the cave somewhere. Scarlett was going to find him, and then the nagging sense of loss that felt like a black hole within her would be gone. It was simply a question of getting to him.

With Caesar as its pilot once again, the boat picked its way between the banks of rocks at the cavern's entrance, until they were almost directly under the statues. The sail was down now, with Tavian and Cruces taking the oars instead to move the boat along. They moved another stroke along, past the entrance.

Something fell into the water behind them with a splash, causing Scarlett to glance back to try to identify it. Judging from where it fell, it must have come from the row of statues above. There was not time to think about that for long though, because beneath them, in the water, something rumbled.

"What's that?" Scarlett asked.

"I do not know," Caesar admitted. "Perhaps…"

The creature burst from the water in a shower of spray, its long, winding body still as thick around as Scarlett was tall. It was a serpent, though one with a head more like that of a lizard than a snake, and with rows of powerful teeth in its jaws rather than just a snake's fangs. A crest of leathery skin surrounded its head, and its scales gleamed an iridescent silvery-blue as more and more of it shot up towards the ceiling.

Then it plunged down.

"Row!" Scarlett yelled, and both Cruces and Tavian hauled on the oars they held. It was barely enough. The plunging head of the serpent missed their boat by mere inches, sending a buffeting swell of spray over the side of the boat.

"It will try to catch us coming up too," Cruces warned, continuing to row hard. "Get ready to…"

The serpent struck them this time. It was only a glancing blow, and Scarlett was glad of that, because those great jaws would easily have been enough to tear their boat apart had they fastened around it. Even so, it was enough to send her staggering, so that Cruces had to grab her wrist to keep her from falling into the water. The serpent plunged down again, missing them once more, though Tavian was able to lash out as it dropped, striking its head with the oar he held.

Perhaps that was what prompted the creature to change tactics. Instead of making another of those breaching and plunging attacks, it rose to the surface slowly, its body forming a series of sinuous curves that mirrored the paths of the waves. Its tail flicked up and then down, striking the water and adding to those waves, so that a swell of sea water threatened to engulf the boat.

160

"We have to turn!" Caesar called out, hauling on the tiller. Scarlett rushed over to help him as best she could, and together, they managed to turn the boat into the wave, so that it would not be swamped. Even so, Cruces and Tavian had to fight to stop the craft from being carried back into one of the walls of the cavern, while the water foamed over the side to drench them all.

The serpent sent two more waves like that, each as big as the last. Each time, Scarlett and Caesar had to use all the strength they had to keep the boat aligned so that it would not capsize. Each time, Cruces and Tavian strained to keep them away from the rocks in the face of the tremendous force of the water.

The serpent dove again then, and for several seconds, Scarlett lost sight of it. She knew it was down in the water somewhere, but she did not know what it had planned. In preparation for the moment when it might attack again, she drew the dagger her parents had given her. Cruces and Tavian seemed to have similar ideas of defending the boat, because they held their oars like quarterstaffs, ready to strike out at the monster should it come close.

It surfaced again, close to the boat. Surrounding the boat, in fact, with the powerful coils of its body forming a ring of scales and muscle around it. Slowly, that ring tightened, and Scarlett guessed what it intended. It meant to crush the boat, and then pick them off one by one once the four of them hit the water.

Scarlett wasn't going to let that happen. She lashed out with her knife the moment the sea serpent was close enough, cutting a wound down its flank that made the beast roar in pain and anger. Cruces struck it with his oar, his vampire strength great enough to snap it. Tavian also struck out, his blows thudding home even though the snake's scaly skin probably prevented most of the damage from getting through to it.

None of that seemed to make any difference though. The blows were powerful, and Scarlett made the creature shriek each time she slashed at it, but they did not stop it from tightening its noose-like embrace around the boat. The serpent wrapped itself tightly around the small vessel, and squeezed despite their best efforts to prevent it. The boat creaked with the strain.

Creaked, and then split. With a scream of tortured wood, the boat started to break apart. Scarlett clung to the side as the deck bucked, slashing at the monster around the boat with her dagger while both Cruces and Tavian continued to attack it with their oars. Cruces actually leaped onto the thing's back, using his broken oar like a spear, yet still it made no difference. The serpent squeezed, and the boat buckled, its timbers splintering as the beast crushed them.

The deck shifted again beneath Scarlett's feet, and this time she could not hold on. She grabbed for the nearest railing, but it gave way in her hand.

"Scarlett!" Tavian yelled, but it made no difference.

Scarlett hit the water in a breathless rush, plunging beneath it before she could do anything to stop it. The water closed around her, and it was all she could do to keep her grip on the dagger. As she plunged down, Scarlett saw that the water here was not deep. The cave provided a natural floor, so that the bottom of it was only fifteen feet below her.

Scarlett came up, gasping for air, and saw that the others were in as much danger as she was. Cruces was still on the serpent's back, but Tavian was in the water too now, clinging to a piece of the broken boat, while Caesar was doing much the same. They called over for Scarlett to join them, but before she could do so, the serpent swung its head towards her and plunged forward.

Scarlett took a breath and dove without thinking about it, and the serpent went past her at a tremendous rate. Cruces was still on it, his spear sticking out of the thing's back near its skull. The vampire hauled on it like he was using it for a rudder, and perhaps it worked, because at least the creature missed Scarlett. Scarlett turned in the water, not gracefully, thanks to her skirts, and made for the surface again. As she did so, however, something on the floor of the cave caught her eye, a flash of white against the basalt floor.

It was only as she surfaced again that Scarlett realized what it had to be. The statue from above the cave. In a flash of inspiration, not even knowing if it would work,

164

she knew what she had to do. Ignoring the shouts of the others to join them, Scarlett filled her lungs with air and dove down.

It was hard getting deep enough. The water seemed to fight her every movement, and her clothing was definitely not made with diving in mind. Yet she knew that she had to be the one to do this. Perhaps the sea serpent sensed that too, because it came at her again. Once again though, Cruces was able to pull on the spear he had embedded in it and force the creature away from Scarlett.

Scarlett forced herself further down, until she made it to the floor of the cavern. The statue was there, gleaming white in the empty water while Scarlett's lungs fought for air. No, not gleaming, glowing. It was the statue that resembled the sea serpent. That was all Scarlett needed. She lifted the knife she held, and with as much force as she could muster through the resistance of the water, she thrust it into the statue.

The sea serpent gave a shriek that Scarlett could hear even under the water. It twisted, turning towards her, its great mouth open. Then a moment later, it was gone, vanished as though it had never been there. The statue under Scarlett's blade, meanwhile, started to crumble into nothing.

Scarlett had more pressing problems. Her lungs burned from the lack of oxygen, and she started to make for the surface, but the weight of her dress made progress even slower going up than it had been reaching the bottom. Scarlett simply did not know if she was going to be able to make it to the brightness of the surface before her lungs overrode her senses and she drowned.

A strong hand clamped onto her forearm, hauling her up out of the water and over the remains of the boat's mast. Scarlett clung to it for dear life while she took in what air she could and gave Tavian a grateful smile.

"Well done," Cruces said, surfacing beside them.

"Well done?" Caesar, also clinging to the mast, looked aghast. "That was my cousin's boat."

"Yes, well, at least you're here to complain about it," the vampire said. "Now I strongly suggest we paddle. There has to be a drier section to this cave somewhere."

Chapter 15

The swim to the shore took them several minutes, clinging to the mast all the while and hoping that there were no more sea creatures there that might wish to eat them. Eventually though, they reached a sloping section of rock that led up out of the water the way a beach would on another island. Scarlett finally felt firm ground beneath her feet as she staggered out of the water. She took a moment to replace her dagger in its thigh sheath, then she, Cruces, Tavian and Caesar sat there for another minute or two trying to dry out, though in the depths of the cave, away from the sun, it wasn't easy to do.

"My cousin isn't going to be happy about his boat," Caesar said.

"I'll buy him a new one," Cruces replied.

That didn't seem to be enough for the stallholder. "Well then, how are we going to get back?"

"We will go back through my world," Scarlett replied, "then jump back to Athens. We would have come here that way if we had known enough about this place to make the trip."

Caesar considered that. "I wish you *had* known. That way, I wouldn't have ended up fighting sea monsters and nearly being drowned by sirens. I'm sure that kind of thing doesn't happen to my cousin."

"Will you shut up about your cousin?" Cruces demanded. "I've already said I'll pay for his boat. Right now, we need to get on with finding Rothschild."

Rothschild. For a moment, in her happiness at surviving the sea serpent, Scarlett had forgotten why they had come there at all. Now, her heart sang with the thought of being so close to the vampire. She had to go to him. She stood quickly, heading for the gap in the rocks. There was a torch there, along with a tinder box that was obviously far too modern for a place like this.

"Wait for the rest of us, Scarlett," Tavian warned. "Don't get too far ahead."

Scarlett nodded as she worked to light the torch, lifting it as it flickered into life. Then, as soon as she was certain that it was not about to go out, she ran deeper into the cave. Rothschild was here somewhere, and Scarlett had no doubt that the others intended him harm, regardless of what they had said about only wanting to help her. As though being in love was some kind of curse to be overcome.

At the same time, they were her friends, and Scarlett did not want them hurt. For all that she loved him, Scarlett knew that Rothschild was not likely to be gentle with either Cruces or Tavian. No, it was far better to leave them all behind now. They would be able to get home once they realized that they would not be able to find Scarlett, Scarlett would be able to warn Rothschild that they were coming, and the two of them would be able to be together in the way that they should be. It was all so simple.

At least, it would be if she could find the vampire. The tunnels through the basalt branched and then branched again, forming something akin to a maze. By touching the mark on her neck, Scarlett thought that she could feel the presence of Rothschild somewhere away over to her right, but that was just a general direction. It told her nothing about how to get through the tunnels that lay between the two of them.

Still, Scarlett did her best, using the light of her torch to guide her way and working from a mixture of guesswork and that nagging sense of where Rothschild was every time she came to a turning. She hurried, knowing that the vampire could not be far away now and wanting to be near him as soon as she could be.

Scarlett stopped sharply, as much on instinct as anything. She did it just in time, as the floor gave way in front of her, falling away to leave a pit so deep that Scarlett could not see the bottom of it even with the torch. Carefully, wary of the slickness of the stone, Scarlett edged her way around to the other side of the pit. She was sure that this was the right way. After all, there would not be traps on dead end routes, would there? Or if there were, they would not be so simply avoided.

Despite the dangers, Scarlett continued on. She was not going to let the threat posed by such things stop her from getting to Rothschild, while even if the vampire had guards protecting him, Scarlett was confident that she could either sneak past them without being detected or convince them that, since she bore Rothschild's mark, they should take her to him. Scarlett would do whatever she needed to in order to see him.

She paused as ahead she spotted a pair of statues facing one another. No, not statues, carvings, cut into the rock of the tunnels. They appeared to be giant stone faces, staring out at one another with open mouths that made them look like they were bellowing in the middle of an argument. That at least proved that the tunnels were not entirely natural. Someone, or something, had cut them into the rock of this island. Had Rothschild played some part in it, or had he simply taken advantage of a place constructed by others?

171

Scarlett approached the statues carefully. Their appearance after so many tunnels of blank rock was too much of a coincidence to ignore. She edged closer, examining them. This close, there was a faint feeling of heat that came from them. On impulse, Scarlett took off one of her still damp shoes and tossed it into the space between the two carved heads.

Flames roared out, waist high, from the mouths of the carvings, shooting out to incinerate her shoe. Another experiment, and the other shoe, confirmed that the flames formed a narrow bar of fire as they shot out. They would have struck Scarlett in the torso had she stepped between the heads, probably killing her instantly.

It took Scarlett a second or two to steel herself for what she knew she had to do next. If she was wrong, then she could well end up killed. Yet the ache that came with the thought of not going to Rothschild was worse than that fear, and Scarlett knew that she would do it, regardless of the danger. She got down on her stomach and crawled, hoping that she was correct.

Scarlett inched between the statutes, and again, fire shot out. Scarlett pressed herself flat to the rock floor,

172

dragging herself forward with her arms. It was slow, terrifyingly so with the fire continuing to pour forth above her. Yet inch by inch, Scarlett made it past the barrier presented by the raging inferno, standing up again only once she was sure that she was clear.

She hurried forward again, keeping a careful eye out for more potential dangers. She quickly found herself in a star shaped room with at least a dozen tunnels branching off it. Which way this time? Scarlett pressed her hand to the mark on her neck, hoping for a clear sense of which way to go. She could feel that Rothschild was ahead somewhere, but that only served to narrow down her options a little. There were still three or four tunnels that could have been the correct one. And, given the dangers in the rest of the cavern complex, Scarlett did not want to risk going the wrong way.

Scarlett looked around the tunnels, trying to pick out some kind of difference between them that would help her to make up her mind. She found it only when she brought the torch close to the floor. She had been hoping for dust or dirt on the floor of the tunnels that might show

173

footprints where others had gone that way. There were no footprints, but there was something almost as good. Most of the tunnels had dust and dirt, exactly as Scarlett expected, but one of them had been swept clean, obviously to obliterate earlier footprints. It was as good as a trail.

Scarlett hurried along it. Behind her, she could hear the sounds of an argument, and even with the echoes of the caves, she could recognize the voices. Cruces and Tavian were following her. Caesar too, from the sounds of it. The sounds of the voices were distorted and channeled by the tunnels, so that Scarlett could not tell exactly how close they were, but it was likely that they could not be far behind.

Briefly, Scarlett thought of going back for them and claiming that her flight was all a mistake. After all, she did not wish her friends to become lost in the caves when to do so might mean so much danger for them. Yet at the same time, Scarlett was only too aware that Cruces and Tavian would probably think she was not acting rationally. They might even insist that they abandon their attempt to get to Rothschild in some misguided attempt to keep her safe.

Being away from Rothschild was not safety. It was an agony of separation that Scarlett simply was not going to allow. She had to get to the vampire before the others caught up with her. In desperation, Scarlett put her hand to the mark she bore, hoping that this time she might be able to get a response.

"Rothschild, please. I am in the caves, coming to you, but I will not be able to find my way quickly enough. The others are not with me now, but they will find me if I do not hurry."

For a second or two there was no response, and Scarlett stood there in despair. Surely Rothschild must be able to hear her so close? He had heard her when she had been close to his home in London, after all. He had to answer. He *had* to.

And then he did.

"Scarlett? You are in the caves? Where?"

Scarlett tried to explain, retracing her route mentally in the hopes that Rothschild would be able to see it. "Cruces and Tavian are behind me, but I think I have managed to get away from them for now."

175

"That is good," Rothschild whispered into her thoughts, "now come to me, dear Scarlett. Come to me."

In that moment, Scarlett knew how to get through the remainder of the tunnels. There was not far to go, and there were no more traps on the way, meaning that even with no shoes, she could run to meet her beloved. Scarlett did not hesitate.

She came out of the tunnels into a cavern that was huge and partly lit by a shaft of sunlight coming from above. The cave was bigger even than the submerged one they had come in through, though this one had a smooth floor of black stone. In the middle of that floor stood a familiar figure.

"Rothschild!" Scarlett started to take a step forward, but a hand clamped onto her arm. She looked around to see Cruces, with Tavian and Caesar behind him. The vampire looked furious.

"You followed me," Scarlett accused.

"Of course we followed you," Cruces said. "What other way was there to end this madness? Rothschild, this is enough. Enough I say!"

Chapter 16

Scarlett put all her strength into breaking free of Cruces' grip, tearing her wrist clear so that she could rush over to Rothschild. She turned to make sure that the others stayed back, glaring at them for following her like that. If they meant Rothschild harm, they would have her to contend with.

Satisfied that Cruces, Tavian and Caesar were staying back for now, Scarlett rushed to Rothschild, kissing him deeply. The vampire ran a hand down her neck, over the mark that sat there. The pleasure from just that movement was enough to make Scarlett half close her eyes for a moment or two.

"I'm sorry," she whispered. "I did not mean to lead them to you. I just could not bear to be parted from you."

"I know," Rothschild said, turning Scarlett gently and hugging her to him from behind. Like that, Scarlett could see the pain on Cruces and Tavian's faces. Couldn't they just be happy for her? Couldn't they accept that this was what Scarlett wanted? No, that was a lie. This was only a small part of everything Scarlett wanted from Rothschild, but it was a beginning, and if the others could not accept even this much, what hope was there for the rest?

"I do believe the great Cruces is jealous," Rothschild murmured beside Scarlett. "Why not tell him who you love, my dear?"

"I love you, Rothschild." Scarlett said it without hesitation.

Cruces took a step forward, a pained expression on his face. "Step away from her, Rothschild. Hand over the bow or face me like a man."

Rothschild sighed. "Oh, how tiresome. No, I do not believe that I will. After all, Scarlett does not wish me to step away from her, do you Scarlett?"

178

Scarlett shook her head. "Please do not fight," she begged. "Cruces, if you harm Rothschild, I will never forgive you for it. I will not allow it."

"You can see how much Scarlett loves me," Rothschild said. He moved beside Scarlett, taking her hand and lifting it like he might kiss it. He turned it over instead, kissing the inside of her wrist, right above the point where her pulse thrummed with excitement. Did he plan to bite her? Scarlett found a strange hint of fear in her at that, but she trusted Rothschild. Trusted him completely in that moment, even as it occurred to Scarlett that he was kissing her there because it was the spot that had borne Cruces' mark.

"Enough," Cruces said once more.

Rothschild straightened up and smiled. "Oh, I don't think so. Not enough by a long way. Scarlett and I are going to get so much closer before I'm done."

"Because of Cupid's bow," Tavian pointed out from beside Cruces. "That is hardly real love, Rothschild."

"You were happy enough when Aphrodite's curse meant I loved you," Scarlett shot back. She saw Tavian

179

wince. She also saw Caesar back away, towards the edge of the room. It could not be easy for him, being caught up in their argument like this.

Cruces made a face. "You are a coward, Rothschild. If you want Scarlett, do the honorable thing. Use the bow to free her from all compulsions."

"Why would I do that?" Rothschild demanded. "Why would I risk that when I am currently so irresistible to our dear Seeker?"

He was irresistible, Scarlett thought. So much so that she could hardly think about anything else.

"If you truly believed that you were irresistible," Cruces pointed out, "you would allow Scarlett the choice. You do not truly believe that you could win her heart by fair means, or you would not hide behind magic."

Rothschild laughed then. "Fair? This is not about whether I am being fair, is it Cruces? You simply cannot stand that once again, a woman has found me more attractive than you. I would have thought you would be used to it by now. After all, it has been that way since our sire made us what we are."

180

"As I remember it," Cruces retorted, "your charm was simply that you never had any restraint."

Scarlett almost laughed at that. *Cruces* was arguing that another vampire lacked control? Given everything that she knew of him, it seemed ludicrous. Yet perhaps he had a point. Rothschild was more dangerous still than him, less inhibited. For all that Cruces was not shy when it came to getting what he wanted, Rothschild simply took it. It was part of what made Rothschild infinitely more attractive to Scarlett in that moment than Cruces could ever be.

Rothschild shook his head. "I would say that if you spent a little less time being responsible you might have a chance with Scarlett. However, that simply wouldn't be true. Would it my dear?"

Scarlett looked up at him with love. She could remember what she had felt for Cruces. She could even remember why she felt the way she did for Rothschild. That changed nothing.

"No. I could never love anyone but you, Rothschild."

"Because of the bow," Tavian said.

181

Cruces nodded. "Isn't this hurting you, Rothschild? You are so proud of your own charms, yet here Scarlett is, held by a compulsion. Wouldn't you rather have her choosing you of her own free will?"

Beside Scarlett, Rothschild shrugged. He pulled Scarlett back to him. "I find that free will is overrated. Scarlett here is precisely the kind of young woman who needs to be compelled. She has too many suitors to ever make the choice for herself, and I will not risk losing her."

"As I said," Cruces snapped. "You are a coward."

Rothschild's grip tightened on Scarlett just a fraction. "Really? I am not the one who has spent time painting me in the worst possible light. You poisoned Scarlett's mind against me as soon as we met, dear brother." He looked at Scarlett then. "You must have hated me when Cruces told you such things about me."

"No... I..." Scarlett wanted to tell him that she could never hate him, but strangely, she could remember a time when she had. She nodded.

Tavian joined in then. "And of course, you need Scarlett to love you so that you can manipulate her into using her gifts to help you. That is what this is about, isn't it Rothschild?"

"Do not presume to know me, boy," Rothschild snapped. "I want Scarlett because of all that she is. Yes, her powers, but the rest of her too. How do you know that I do not love her as much as she loves me now?"

"You love no one but yourself, Rothschild," Cruces said. Scarlett noted that he'd started to circle, obviously looking for a way past Scarlett to get to Rothschild. Scarlett moved to keep herself between them.

"This from you, Cruces?" Rothschild demanded.

"Isn't it true?" Cruces stalked around them another pace. "Show me a time and a place where you have genuinely cared about someone. Where you have not just used your looks to take what you want until you have become bored and cast your conquests aside."

Scarlett's heart constricted at that. "You would not cast *me* aside, would you?"

Rothschild silenced her with a kiss. "Never."

183

"Never?" Cruces scoffed. "Then what about Cecilia? How long did you promise to stay with that foolish girl? How well did you keep your word there, Rothschild?"

"Be silent, Cruces."

The vampire shook his head. "Scarlett is, despite the adventures of her life, both pure and innocent. Yet you are going to ruin that for your own ends. And I fear it will bring disaster. How do you know that the very purity you have corrupted with this magic is not what allows her to use her powers?"

"Nonsense," Rothschild said, but Scarlett couldn't help noticing that he loosened his grip on her a little. "It cannot be true."

"Why not?" Cruces asked. "There have been stories throughout time of young women who had power only so long as they retained that innocence. Are you truly willing to risk it?"

Scarlett turned away from Cruces then, throwing herself at Rothschild once more. She was not about to let Lord Darthmoor separate them with his words. She was not going to let him put doubt into the mind of the man she loved. Scarlett looked up into Rothschild's eyes.

184

"I love you," she said simply. "Do not listen to him. I will do anything for you."

"If you do love her," Cruces said, "there is one other thing to consider. That is not Scarlett. Oh, she looks the same. Her hair is as golden, her form as lovely, her features as beautiful. It is not her, nonetheless."

"Do not be foolish," Rothschild snarled.

"I am not being foolish. What attracted you to Scarlett?" Cruces looked his vampire brother in the eye. "Was it merely beauty? We have both had many beautiful women through the centuries. No. Scarlett is more than that. She has wit. She has fire. Or she had it, at any rate. Now, she is too besotted with you to do more than simper. Is that what you want? Well, do you?"

Rothschild smiled. "I happen to think that Scarlett is very alluring this way. And I *know* that you have no objection to your women empty headed and doting, Cruces. What about you, gypsy boy? Or you, the newcomer? Who here does not find Scarlett at least as attractive now that she is willing to do anything for the man she loves?"

185

Scarlett looked up at Rothschild. She wanted to argue with that, because even though she loved him, it did not mean that he could say such things about her. Yet doing so might make him angry. Might make him stop loving her. No, Scarlett could not risk that.

Away in the shadows at the edge of the cavern, a sound began. It took Scarlett a moment or two to place it, and even when she did, it made little sense. It was the sound of someone applauding slowly and sarcastically. It kept going until everyone there was looking in the direction the sound had come from.

A voice followed. It was a woman's voice, and it was beautiful, but there was a streak of authority running through it that lent it a harsher edge, suggesting that there was little kindness to be found there.

"Oh, my brothers. Arguing as usual over your toys. All these years and the two of you still haven't grown up that much? Disappointing."

A woman stepped from the shadows. She was beautiful, but over the past few days Scarlett had seen many beautiful women. What set this one apart was the sense of authority she exuded. She walked like she expected adoration at every step, and would take it if she did not get it. Her hair was dark and fell midway down her back, matching the loose dress she wore. Something about her features reminded Scarlett strongly of Cruces. Scarlett got the feeling that the newcomer was looking directly at her.

"And Rothschild, why is it that you must always reduce your women to such foolish, vacuous dolls?"

"Rothschild, Cruces?" Scarlett asked. "Who is that?"

Rothschild sighed. "That is Lydia. Our sister."

187

Chapter 17

Lydia stalked forward, and even Scarlett had to admit that she was beautiful. It was not, perhaps, the impossible beauty of Aphrodite, but it was there nonetheless. It was a cruel beauty though. It was not one that would have men throwing themselves at her so much as admiring her from afar and possibly secretly hoping that the vampire might call them closer. The resemblance to Cruces also had Scarlett thinking.

"She's actually your sister, isn't she?" Scarlett said. "Biologically, as well as the way that dear Rothschild is your brother."

Across from them, Lydia shook her head sadly. "You were doing so well until the 'dear Rothschild' part, too. As I said, Rothschild always makes such stupid dolls of his playthings. Yes, I am Cruces' sister. Though he has long since forgotten what vampires are for."

"I have not forgotten," Cruces said. Scarlett noted that he moved into something close to a defensive stance. Apparently, he did not trust his sister. "I have simply learned a better way."

Lydia shook her head and stopped moving forward. She had moved into the spot where the light shone down behind her perfectly, forcing those there to pay attention to her. Somehow, Scarlett knew it was deliberate. "There *is* no other way than the one the immortals decreed for us."

"So you say," Cruces said.

"So I know. We were to be the instruments of fear among humanity, reminding them of their place in the great order of things. We were to make them cry out for the aid of the gods and goddesses. That is what we are. What we were made for."

"But it does not have to be all that we ever are," Cruces said softly. Had he had this conversation with his sister before? His tone made it sound like it was a well-

189

worn argument. One that neither would give ground on. "When I became the Keeper, I learned to love them, to want to keep them safe."

"I remember when you used to be more than that," Lydia countered. She sounded not just sad now, but angry. "You used to fulfill your purpose. Our sire was not pleased to hear of your betrayals."

Cruces shrugged. "I helped humans, and in doing so, I did what I believed to be right, Lydia. Can you say as much?"

Lydia paused. She did not back down, though. "I do what I was created to do, brother. I do what we were all created to do. It is all I can do."

Beside Scarlett, Rothschild sighed, and this close, Scarlett could feel his annoyance spilling into her like a wave. "You know, there's a reason I dislike family reunions. Nobody ever sticks to the point. What are you doing here, Lydia?"

The female vampire spread her hands elegantly. On anyone else, the gesture might have seemed innocent and open. Somehow though, Scarlett doubted that she had ever been those things.

"Can a sister not see her brothers?" Lydia asked.

"Lydia." From Cruces it was deeper, more threatening. "Tell us why you have come here. We have not seen you in long years, yet now, here you are. Tell us."

"Very well," the female vampire said. "I have come because I have been instructed to do so. Unlike the two of you, I still do what I am instructed."

"And what else have you been instructed to do?" Cruces asked carefully.

"First, I have been instructed to retrieve the bow. Hand it over, Rothschild."

"Let's assume that I'm going to say no to that," Rothschild replied. Scarlett noticed that even before he said it, the bow flashed back into its form as Gordon's stick. The glamor didn't seem like much protection for it there and then, but perhaps it was better than nothing.

"You would keep it from me?" Lydia asked. "Even though we are on the same side?" She held out her hand, as though expecting Rothschild to simply step forward and pass the bow to her. "I have no wish to harm you, brother."

"You should know by now that I'm mostly on *my* side," Rothschild said. "And you said 'first'. What is second?"

"Ah, yes." Lydia nodded to the side of the cavern, where the light did not reach so strongly, and the shadows gathered in deep clusters.

Scarlett turned to look, as did almost everyone else. Because of that, she was just in time to see the limp form of Caesar tumble from the shadows. His throat was gone. Simply gone, in a red ruin that was hard to look at. He collapsed to the floor, already dead by the time he hit it. Scarlett stared at his body for a second or two, barely able to comprehend the suddenness of his death. Just a short while ago, he had been helping them to paddle to shore, while complaining that his cousin would be angry about the loss of his boat. Now, Caesar would never see his cousin again.

Scarlett was still thinking of that feeling a faint feeling of sadness and guilt when the shadows themselves seemed to leap forward in human shape. No, not human. Vampire. Scarlett could feel that as surely as she could feel the presence of Rothschild beside her. The creature was tall

192

and slender, seemingly composed of the shadows themselves. It slid around the darkest recesses of the cave, and then bounded straight at Scarlett almost quicker than the eye could follow. Rothschild half turned to intercept it, and was knocked to the ground for his trouble. Tavian went sprawling into the nearest wall. The creature reared over Scarlett, seeming to blot out the light. Only two deep red eyes broke the darkness of it

Cruces hit it, slamming into it from the side with a roar of rage. The creature didn't seem to notice as Cruces passed through it like smoke, yet when it turned, slashing with hands that were more like claws, three gouges briefly opened up on Cruces' chest. Cruces struck back, and again, it was like he was punching mist. His hand passed through the creature completely, only for the return blow to knock Cruces back a pace.

"What are you?" Cruces asked. Scarlett could hear the fear in his voice, though her concern right then was with helping Rothschild back to his feet.

193

"Don't you recognize him, brother?" Lydia asked. "He is one of us. A vampire of the Order. Or he was, until you and yours slew him."

She would have said more, but Tavian chose that moment to attack the shadowy vampire. Scarlett thought that it would be as futile as Cruces' attempts, but Tavian drew on his fey heritage as he attacked, wrapping glamor around himself so that for an instant or two, he appeared as the vampire did. The strike he threw made the shadowy creature cry out in pain, and Scarlett knew that somehow, he had succeeded in connecting where Cruces could not.

His success was not total though. The power needed to use glamor as a weapon like that was clearly immense, because Tavian's glamor flickered and shifted, there only in brief bursts of effort. When it was not in place, all Tavian could do was dodge and duck, trying to avoid the strikes thrown his way while he recovered enough concentration to attack once more.

"Who is it?" Cruces asked his sister again.

Lydia smiled sadly. "You should not have left the Order, Cruces. We have advanced a great deal since you did. We have been focused in our search for Devices,

194

unlike Rothschild here." She looked over to where Scarlett clung to Rothschild. "One brother who has forgotten what he should be, and both made weak by desire. Such foolishness."

"You still haven't answered the question," Scarlett pointed out. "Who, or what, is that creature?"

That earned her a brief smile. "So, you can think beyond how much you love our dear brother. Interesting. The short answer is that we have a Device that can connect with the ethereal. With it, a dead vampire need not stay that way, not entirely."

In that moment, the shadowy vampire battling Tavian stepped away and spoke. "Cruces, you should not have left the Order. It was because of you I perished, even if it was at the girl's hands."

Cruces looked as dumbfounded as Scarlett felt in that moment. "Elder?" Cruces asked. The shadowy vampire did not answer, but plunged back into combat with Tavian instead. The fey-blooded young man barely deflected a rapid series of strikes, while his own efforts were parried easily.

195

"It cannot be Elder," Cruces said. "I saw him die."

"You saw me die once, to become this," Lydia pointed out. "The idea of living beyond a death should not be so hard for you. This is simply Elder's... ghost, if you will."

"But vampires do not have ghosts," Scarlett said. She of all people should know. She had seen so many ghosts in her life, after all. None of them had been the ghosts of vampires. So how could this one be? Not understanding, Scarlett turned to Rothschild. If anyone knew, it would be him.

"That is impossible," Rothschild said.

"Oh, it is possible," Lydia retorted, bringing out a silver box. On it were etched designs that featured skulls and funerary artifacts. "Let us test our Seeker. Do you know what this is? Come, take your eyes from my brother long enough to look."

Scarlett wanted to retort that she was not mindless, but it was in fact a struggle not to look at Rothschild. She stared at the box. "It is a Device. It must be the one you mentioned."

"There, that wasn't so hard." Lydia lifted the box. "A simple thing, with the ashes of dead vampires inside. Those who hold it control the shade it brings up. Allow me to demonstrate."

She glanced over to where Elder and Tavian still fought, and the ghost of the vampire kicked Tavian back from itself.

"Where did you find it?" Rothschild asked. "I had searched for it, but concluded that it was merely a legend."

Lydia laughed at that. "Well, perhaps if you did not spend quite so much time causing trouble in England and chasing after young women, you might have found it instead. You might even have gotten to it before me, though I doubt that. I was always a few steps ahead of you both, brothers. I think I will stay that way, too."

Scarlett could feel Rothschild's anger through the connection they had. This time, it was barely restrained.

"No," Rothschild said. "I have Scarlett now. She will help me find the rest before you do."

197

"No," Lydia said, with a shake of her head and an almost apologetic look at Scarlett. "She won't. She will not get the chance."

Lydia disappeared then. Simply disappeared. It took Scarlett a moment to realize that she must have used her ring to leap between worlds. By the time Scarlett realized that, Lydia was back, only she did not reappear in quite the same place. Instead, Scarlett found her neck being wrenched back into a taut line as Lydia seized her from behind.

"I am sorry," the vampire said, her mouth opening to reveal the fangs that would flash down to end Scarlett's life.

Chapter 18

Rothschild struck out at Lydia before the vampire's fangs could touch Scarlett, knocking her back with such force that she slammed into the cave wall in a shower of dust and fell to one knee, her features torn and bruised by the impact. Rothschild started forward, his hands clenching into fists.

"How dare you?" Rothschild demanded, in a tone that was practically a roar of anger. "Scarlett is mine. My woman, bearing my mark. Striking at her is striking at me. You know that attacking one marked by another is forbidden."

"Forbidden?" Lydia straightened up, reaching behind her head and frowning as she spotted a smear of blood on her hand. It was the kind of frown a housewife in London might have given on finding that the maid had missed a spot when dusting. Her features were badly bruised from the force of Rothschild's attack, yet even as Scarlett watched, those bruises faded. Vampires were not slowed by such minor injuries. "Nothing is forbidden by a mark, Rothschild. It merely means that the vampire making an attack must be prepared to fight the one who placed the mark there. And I am more than prepared to fight, if that becomes necessary."

Rothschild bristled. "If? Scarlett bears my *mark,* Lydia. You think I will not fight for her?"

Lydia smiled sadly. "I think that you will not succeed if you do. Be wise, brother. Accept that the Seeker was always meant to be fair game for all of us. She bore the Order's mark before you placed your own within it. I have the right to do as I have been commanded, and if you will not recognize that… well, I will do what I must."

Rothschild shook his head. "Scarlett might have borne the Order's mark first, but I *did* place mine within it. She is mine now, by my mark and by the rest of it. Aren't you Scarlett?"

200

Scarlett nodded. She was Rothschild's. Even without the mark, it was in her heart. They were meant to be together. She loved him, totally and completely. She did not think that she would be able to live without him.

"I hardly think her opinion matters here," Lydia said. She stretched like a cat, apparently checking that the damage done to her was gone.

"What about mine then, Lydia?" Cruces demanded. His voice was as firm as before, but there was something almost pleading about it. He clearly did not want to fight. "I marked Scarlett even before the Order."

Lydia shook her head. "You know that does not matter, my brother. Marks... well, they are a question of honor, they always were. There is little enough honor left in the Order. There is no honor among thieves, as they say, and we are far worse than thieves these days."

"You don't sound happy about it," Scarlett said. The vampire woman looked over to her as though only just remembering that Scarlett was there. "Why not leave?"

"Perhaps I *do* have some honor," Lydia said. She looked over to Cruces. "I keep my word, unlike some."

201

Cruces shrugged. "I have seen what the Order has become," he said. "I have seen enough that I am happy to be without honor if it means being no part of that."

"You should not have left," Lydia said. "We have all missed you, Cruces. I have missed you. It simply wasn't the same, but we have grown. The anger at your leaving has given the Order strength. You have not weakened it. You have fueled it."

Cruces looked pained at that. Scarlett wondered what it would be like, having a sibling still caught up in something like that. A sibling who was apparently happy to be a part of it, or who at least seemed to be proud of remaining within it.

"You should leave the Order, Lydia." Cruces took a step towards his sister as he said it, though whether it was to comfort her or seize her, Scarlett didn't know.

"No," Lydia snapped. "I will not abandon what we are meant to be so easily. I will not betray us like that. We are vampires, Cruces. We are stronger than humans, faster than humans. We are meant to be feared. We are meant to rule and force the weak to run to the immortals. We do not get the choice of abandoning that."

"There is always a choice, Lydia."

"A choice to fall in love with one of the weak?" the female vampire demanded with a vicious look at Scarlett. "It used to be that you would not even pretend to such a thing unless you meant to turn the mortal. Now look at you. Come back to us, Cruces. Be strong again. Teach the humans and the fey their place in the world."

Cruces shook his head. "I am strong, Lydia. Strong enough to know that you should not do this."

"Perhaps. We will see." Lydia seemed to be done talking. She nodded to the shadowy ghost of Elder, and the thing threw itself forward. Tavian moved to intercept it, using his glamor to protect himself once more. The attack was ferocious, but with Tavian able to change himself to match the creature, it could make little real progress against him. It would swing a punch, and Tavian would dodge, then strike back with his hands as shadowy as the ghost's, forcing it to defend in turn.

Neither was winning. Every blow that was thrown was parried in turn. Every counter was blocked. Tavian's glamor was still not strong enough to maintain the shadow

203

form in full, but it was enough to let him stay in the fight. While he did that, Rothschild leaped at Lydia, but the female vampire avoided the attack, darting to the side and away. Cruces tried to join the assault on his sister, moving to try to grab her, but again she skipped away, this time running along the nearest wall to do it. Both vampires jumped at her at once, and she briefly disappeared using her ring, only to reappear near Scarlett again, forcing Rothschild and Cruces to focus on defending her.

Tavian and the ghost of Elder were still fighting, and slowly, it was becoming apparent that the ghost had the upper hand. Tavian was still using his glamor to strike back at the creature, but that was happening less and less often. While the ghost had the strength of un-death behind it, Tavian was starting to tire. Even as Scarlett watched, Tavian stumbled to one knee, while the ghost moved in for the kill.

Cruces and Rothschild could not help. They were both busy trying to keep Lydia at bay. The vampire kept darting in, testing their defenses, then flitting away again. Scarlett would have to be the one to do something. So she did. She reached down and drew her dagger, before leaping forward.

The ghost of Elder was so intent upon Tavian that it never saw her coming. Scarlett plunged her dagger into it, the same way she had used the blade to kill the creature when it had been alive. Perhaps it was the memory of that moment that made the ghost shriek quite so loudly was the blade plunged home. It was not memory, however, that made the blade feel like it was burning in Scarlett's hand. It was not memory that sent motes of golden light flashing through the shadows that made up the creature. It was not memory that made the creature cry out one final time before scattering into shreds and scraps of shadow.

"No!" Lydia cried out, looking over. "How have you done that, you pathetic little… the dagger. They did not tell me that you had a weapon like that." Lydia dodged again as Rothschild lunged at her.

"Give up, Lydia," Cruces said. "Give up or flee back to the Order. You have failed here."

"Failed?" For a moment, the vampire looked slightly stunned by that idea. Then she shook her head firmly. "No. This is not over. I still have a task to perform. You think that Elder is the only destroyed vampire in the world?"

Lydia's eyes gleamed evilly as she reached into a pocket of her dress, withdrawing a small pouch. She raised the silver box that had brought back Elder, the lid open and waiting. Scarlett watched, and she was so busy watching that she did not even complain when Tavian drew her back into his arms. He was not Rothschild, but right then, Scarlett could feel the tension in the cave growing until the air itself felt like it was stretched tight.

"Whatever vampire you are thinking of bringing back," Cruces said, "we will defeat it."

"Vampire?" Lydia laughed. "You think I am bringing back *one* vampire?"

Somehow, instinctively, Scarlett knew that what the vampire was intending was a terrible idea. Perhaps it was simply that she could sense something of the power of the item Lydia held. Scarlett reached out imploringly. "Lydia, no!"

Lydia ignored Scarlett's cry and upended the bag she held into the silver box.

For a second or two nothing happened. Scarlett did not relax though. She did not dare to think that they might have been lucky enough for Lydia's attempt not to work. The item the vampire held was a Device, after all, and those were far too powerful to fail so simply. The others there must have sensed the same danger, because they stood just as still as Scarlett did.

The light dimmed in the cave, as though the shaft of sunlight above had found itself blocked by a cloud. Scarlett knew that was not it, however. A cloud did not account for the sudden feeling of power rushing through the air. Nor did it explain the way the temperature in the cave dropped so that, despite the heat outside, Scarlett felt herself shivering.

Footsteps sounded in the tunnel leading to the cave. At least, Scarlett assumed that they had come from there. In truth, the sound seemed to come from all around so that Scarlett could not truly place it. There were so many footsteps too. It sounded like a brigade marching by. An army. The shadows deepened still further for a moment, before giving way to sunlight again. Scarlett saw them then.

"The shadows!"

There were dozens of them. More. Too many to easily count, given the way they shifted back and forth, blurring through one another in a constant web of motion. There were large figures and small ones, male and female ones, all seemingly composed of nothing but shadow. They were in the cave, and they were advancing towards its walls. They climbed up them with all the speed and silence of spiders, climbing away into the shadows above them so that Scarlett could not see where they went. She only knew that they were up there somewhere, watching, scuttling, and picking out their prey.

Then, with a cry that seemed to come from all of them at once, the ghosts of the vampires dropped.

Chapter 19

Scarlett gasped as the ghosts of the vampires landed around them in a circle. Cruces echoed it. "What have you done, Lydia?" Cruces demanded. "Do you even know what you have done, summoning so many? Summoning *these* vampires?"

"I have done what I must to achieve the Order's ends," Lydia said. "You had your chance to give me the bow, Cruces."

"You *don't* know," Cruces said. "These vampires… I recognize some of those shapes. They were mad when they were alive. In death, you will never control them."

"I have the box," Lydia said confidently.

Scarlett shook her head. "There are too many. I can feel it. There are too many to control."

"You're trying to trick me," Lydia snapped, "and it won't work. Spirits, kill them."

Lydia had to dive back as one of the shadows swiped at her. Scarlett saw the female vampire's eyes widen in surprise and fear, but they had other concerns right then. The ring of shadowy vampires was closing in on them.

"There are too many of them," Tavian said.

"I can get to them with my dagger if you create a distraction," Scarlett replied, hefting the weapon. She had killed Elder's ghost easily enough, after all.

Cruces put a restraining hand on Scarlett's wrist, then pulled her aside as one of the shadows leaped. It looked puzzled to have missed her. Meanwhile Lydia was having to dodge her way through a small mob of the creatures.

"We cannot fight them outright," Cruces said. "As much as I admire your bravery, Scarlett, we would be torn to shreds. These vampires are feral, plus they have all the

210

advantages of their ghostly form. I doubt Tavian can fight them all off as he did with Elder."

"No," Tavian agreed, "but I can create the illusion of it. The shadows won't know which ones we are."

"So we kill each other by accident?" Rothschild demanded.

"I will mark us out with a red spot. It will be easy."

"There's no time to think of anything better," Cruces said, ducking as another vampire leaped. "When the glamor wears off, meet me wherever I am. I will get us out of here. I'd do it now, but we need that box."

Scarlett nodded. She kept her eyes on Rothschild. She was not going to let herself be separated from him again. Rothschild's eyes were on Lydia, who still held the box as she avoided the surrounding vampires, trying to command them even as they attacked her. The vampires around the four of them, meanwhile, had started to close in.

"Now, Tavian," Cruces said.

Tavian nodded, and a second later, he, Cruces and Rothschild disappeared, to be replaced with shadow forms. Scarlett looked down and saw that she had been transformed too. She moved forward, slashing with her dagger whenever a shadow got too close. The aim was not to destroy them, but simply to cut a path through them to Lydia.

Some of the shadows seemed to notice that others of their number were attacking them, and tried to fight back. One threw Scarlett to the ground, but Tavian tripped it, giving Scarlett enough time to thrust her dagger into it and end its existence. Cruces, meanwhile, played on the confusion among the shadows, darting between them until he had them attacking one another with savage ferocity. The shadowy vampires had fangs several inches long, and they tore at one another like wild beasts. Scarlett took advantage of the opportunity to stab another one, watching it dissolve into shreds of darkness.

A pair of shadowy hands grabbed Scarlett, and she cried out in surprise as the glamor around her slipped away.

"I see you," the vampire said. "I see you, and I hunger."

The vampire looked as though it might tear her apart. It opened its mouth wide, displaying its fangs. That was as far as it got though, because in that moment, another fell on it, fighting with it brutally. Another joined the brawl, and another. Scarlett started as she realized the creatures were fighting over her. They were so maddened by their hunger that they would kill each other just for that much blood.

"Scarlett!" Tavian's voice came from close beside her. He was still glamored, still appearing as one of the shadows. "Come with me!"

He grabbed her and dragged her out of the frenzy, but the others would not allow what appeared to be one of their number to steal away their prey so easily. Scarlett had to stab another with the dagger, and Tavian had to swipe at two more with claws made of shadow, before they were able to break free of the main group.

In clear space at last, Scarlett was able to look around.

"Where's Cruces?" Scarlett asked. Why she asked about him first, she did not know. She only knew that she was suddenly very much aware he was missing, as well as worried about his fate. Around her, the shadow vampires

213

were tearing one another apart in a futile effort to get some kind of sustenance.

Tavian shook his head. "It doesn't matter," he said. "Let's get out of here. It's too dangerous. They are tearing each other apart, and we don't want to be in the middle of it."

"Scarlett!" another voice shouted. Cruces' voice. It came from one end of the cave, out towards the tunnels leading to it. "Join me now!"

Scarlett and Tavian started to make their way towards that voice, but Scarlett knew that she could not do it. "Where's Rothschild?" she demanded, stopping completely. Tavian tried to pull her towards Cruces, but Scarlett did not move. "I am not leaving without Rothschild."

She looked around for him and finally spotted him a little way away, struggling with Lydia. His glamor had fallen away and now he struggled with her, trying to grab the silver box even as Lydia tried to get her hands on the stick that had been Cupid's bow. They struggled hand to hand, neither able to make any headway as they both tried to keep away from the rampaging shadows.

214

Even as Scarlett watched, though, that changed. Rothschild let go his grip on the box and reached inside his coat to draw out a wooden stake. He slammed it into Lydia's chest, then stepped back to admire his work as he took the box from her.

"You missed my heart," Lydia said.

"Perhaps I was not trying to hit it." Rothschild lifted the silver box and poured the ashes from it. It appeared to make no difference to the shadow vampires.

The female vampire shook her head. "You should have."

With Rothschild's hands occupied by both the bow and the box, he could not defend himself as Lydia drew the stake out of herself and slammed it into him. Rothschild's eyes went wide with pain. Scarlett gasped as a fraction of it seared along the mark that lay between them, and her eyes met his.

I love you. The words came directly into her head, thanks to the mark. He threw the cane, and it arced above the fighting vampires for a moment. Cruces reached up and it smacked squarely into his palm as he caught it.

215

"Take care of her," Rothschild called out, tipping his hand so that the last ashes in the box fell from it. "Destroy the Order."

"Traitor!"

Rothchild groaned as Lydia thrust the stake deeper, and Scarlett screamed. It felt like the stake was plunging into her own chest. The vampire vanished, scattering into silvery dust that floated down to mingle with that he had poured out onto the floor.

"No!" Scarlett struggled to go to Rothschild, hitting out at Cruces and Tavian even as they held her back. She kicked Tavian sharply, knowing that she had to go to Rothschild. To get to his remains. Or perhaps... yes, she still had the dagger. One thrust and she could join him. One simple thrust, and...

"Hold her, Tavian!" Cruces stepped back, lifted the stick he held and it was a bow once more. He drew the string back and fired what seemed to be an arrow of the dullest grey into Scarlett. She froze for a moment, then stood there shaking her head. What had she been thinking. What had she been about to do?

"She is herself again?" Tavian asked.

216

"I hope so," Cruces said.

More of the shadow vampires moved towards them then, and Tavian took a step forward.

"Go," he said, "I can hold them."

"You're sure?" Cruces stepped forward to shake Tavian's hand. It seemed an oddly noble gesture, under the circumstances, and a stupid one.

"What?" Scarlett demanded. "You're planning to stay here?"

It was too late to say anything else. Tavian was already fighting off vampires. Cruces, meanwhile, had grabbed Scarlett around the waist. In an instant, they were in the space between worlds, moving away from the Ancient Greece of myth too fast to follow. They appeared in front of Cruces' house, right on the doorstep. Scarlett tried to pull away.

"Tavian!" Scarlett cried. "We can't leave him behind."

"Hush," Cruces said, "Tavian will be alright."

"No, he'll be stuck there. We have to go back, I'm not leaving my Tavian behind."

217

Cruces groaned. "Your Tavian? Oh, for pity's sake! Don't tell me that I have undone the effects of the bow only for Aphrodite's meddling to take hold. There is nothing to see here," he snapped to a couple of passersby.

"We must go back," Scarlett insisted.

Cruces shook his head. "We cannot."

"Why can't we?" Scarlett demanded. "Either take me back or unhand me."

"I want to talk to you Scarlett," Cruces said. "I want you to know… I think you were able to get through to Rothschild. He would not have stood against Lydia like that purely for the sake of the Devices. Not unless he understood how important humanity was. He has not understood that in thousands of years though, so there is only one explanation. You changed him, at the end. You Scarlett."

Scarlett was not sure about that. She could remember her foolish forced love for Rothschild, an emotion that stood as nothing now, so that she could even remember the moment of Rothschild's death without pain.

"I am sorry for your loss, Cruces. He was, after all, your brother." Scarlett paused. "Please, go back for Tavian."

"No," Cruces said.

"Why not?"

Cruces kissed her then, ignoring Scarlett's brief protest. How dare he?

"Scarlett, please. You'll see him soon enough. Right now, I just want this moment alone with you, even if it is on my doorstep. You may not remember, but at one point you cared for me. I could feel it when we kissed. You and I. The Seeker and the Keeper. We are meant to be."

As Cruces kissed her again, just for a moment, Scarlett thought that she could feel it. She could feel the need for him. The moment after that though, as they broke apart, it was gone. Scarlett stood back, and Cruces opened the door to let them inside.

Chapter 20

They went inside, with Cruces more or less pulling Scarlett after him. They headed into the dining room, where the vampire looked around impatiently, then looked at his pocket watch.

"I didn't think we'd have to wait. That's why I brought us back outside. Still, any second now, I should think. Ah, here we go."

Scarlett watched open-mouthed as the air in the room split open to allow Tavian to step through. The young fey man had scrapes on his cheeks from the fight he'd been in, but otherwise he seemed to be all right. Scarlett's gasp of amazement was not so much at the sudden appearance, since she knew perfectly well by now that travel between worlds could happen, but at the fact Tavian could do it at all, when Cruces was here with the ring that allowed it.

"Tavian," Scarlett breathed. "He's really here?"

"You can see him, Scarlett," Cruces said with surprising gentleness, reaching out to touch Scarlett's chin with his fingertips. For once, Scarlett did not pull back. "I told you that he would be joining us, and I keep my word."

Even so, Scarlett moved over to Tavian, reaching out to touch him just to see if he was really there.

"It's really you?" Scarlett asked, but the love inside her as Aphrodite's spell welled up answered that.

"It's really me," Tavian promised.

"How?" Scarlett asked, looking back at Cruces, trying to understand. "If we left him behind, how can he be here?"

Tavian reached out to turn Scarlett gently back to him, and as his hand touched her cheek, Scarlett felt the cold presence of metal. She took Tavian's hand and looked down at it. There, clear in the light coming through the window, was Cruces' ring. Scarlett thought back, suddenly understanding. She looked over at Cruces.

221

"When you shook hands, you gave Tavian your ring."

Cruces nodded. "I had just seen the pain that losing someone you loved that deeply could cause you, so I could not risk his loss. I will not have you hurt like that, Scarlett. Besides, we will need our young gypsy's help if we are to retrieve Gordon and, yes, Cecilia later on." Cruces smiled. "In any case, regardless of what I might feel, I know that Tavian is one of the few others in this world who will do whatever he must to keep you safe. That is valuable to me, Scarlett. Valuable enough to be worth one magical ring, at least."

Scarlett stayed silent at that. The scope of the gift was not lost on her. Nor were the feelings behind it. That Cruces would give up a way of travelling between worlds to ensure that Scarlett remained safe said a lot. Too much, perhaps, given what she currently felt for Tavian. It also begged one very important question.

"If Tavian has your ring, how did we get back?" she asked. "How did we manage to travel between worlds?"

Cruces looked momentarily pained. "Rothschild. His ring was around the shaft of the walking stick when he threw it to me. I think he knew what would be needed to keep you safe, or perhaps he simply did not wish Lydia and those who command her to have another item of such power." Cruces sighed. "I will miss him. He plotted, and schemed, and occasionally killed, but he was a brother to me for so long that I can't help missing him. And there was some good in him at the end."

The vampire fell into silence then, obviously remembering, and Scarlett wanted to go to him. She wanted to put her arm around him. She wanted to kiss him. Scarlett started, surprised that she would want that when it was Tavian she loved, but right then, she *did* want to kiss Cruces. She could feel that need bubbling up inside her like a wellspring. For the moment, however, Scarlett had to squash that feeling. Tavian was there, and she loved him regardless of what else she felt. She was not about to complicate that in such a way.

After a moment or two, Cruces straightened up and rang through for his butler. George appeared neatly and efficiently.

"Tea for my guests, George," he said, "four cups please. Plus wine from my reserve for myself, obviously."

"Four cups, sir?" the butler asked, looking to Scarlett and Tavian in turn.

"There will be more guests along shortly, I imagine."

"Very good, sir."

Scarlett raised an eyebrow. "More guests? Who are you expecting, Cruces?"

Cruces nodded to two of the chairs in the room. "Them."

Aphrodite and Hephaestus appeared in the chairs almost exactly as Cruces said the word, arriving in a blaze of light that almost made Scarlett look away. When it passed, the couple appeared as they had before, beautiful and clad in golden cloth, looking absolutely perfect. They had with them a golden-haired boy who appeared to be about ten or so, dressed the same way they were, and with an expression that made it clear he hadn't wanted to come.

"But Mother," the boy was saying, "I have already promised Alexander that I will go around to his house, and…"

"Enough, Cupid," Aphrodite said. "We're here now."

Cupid looked around. "Well, this looks boring."

Aphrodite looked over to Cruces with an almost pleading expression. "Please tell me that you have the bow. No, I know you do, I can feel it. Hand it over. My son is turning into a mortal brat far too quickly for anyone's good."

"I am *not*."

Beside his wife, Hephaestus let out a sigh and looked to Scarlett. "Aphrodite is right. You have succeeded in your quest, our champion. All that remains is to return the bow to where it should be."

Cruces shook his head. "Not so fast."

"Not so *fast?*" Aphrodite repeated. "Don't you remember what happened the last two times you irritated me, vampire?"

"I remember all too well," Cruces retorted, "which is why I want to make sure that you are going to keep your word. You did not see how things were in my home."

"We did," Cupid said. "Mother used one of the reflecting pools on Olympus to look."

Scarlett bit her lip then. She hated the thought that she and the others had been used for simple entertainment by these immortals. Before she could say anything, thankfully, George the butler returned with the drinks. Scarlett took the time to sip her tea and compose her thoughts.

Hephaestus appeared to be doing the same. "We watched you because we were concerned for our son," he said. "We wanted to be certain that our mortal champion was going to complete the task in time to help Cupid. And you, Cruces, have *my* word that my wife's spell will be lifted." He raised a hand when Scarlett started to interrupt. "I know, my dear. You do not feel like you are bespelled. You simply feel as though you are in love. Even so, we should not interfere in what you genuinely feel."

"Really?" Aphrodite snapped. "Why not? I am a goddess of love, not of standing around doing nothing."

"So you will not stand around doing nothing while our son turns into one of them then, will you?" Hephaestus demanded, and for a moment the air was tense between the two of them. Eventually though, Aphrodite looked away.

"Oh, very well," she said. "But they hand over the bow first. I'm not having Cupid stay like this for a second longer than he has to."

Cruces looked like he might argue with that, but Scarlett reached out to put a hand on his arm. "Give him the bow, Cruces," she said.

"You're sure?"

Scarlett nodded. "Someone here has to show some trust. It might as well be us."

Cruces nodded and handed the bow, which had reverted to being a stick yet again, over to Cupid. The boy took it as though he could barely understand what it was he was taking hold of. Briefly, Scarlett found herself wondering if it was too late. Was Cupid condemned to being an ordinary mortal boy, destined to grow up, get old, and eventually die?

Then the stick in Cupid's hands started to glow then, becoming the bow once more, and he started to glow. He glowed as brightly as a miniature sun, but then seemed to almost pull the light back into himself, claiming the power and controlling it. Scarlett stared at the boy there for a second or two afterwards, and even in that short space the difference was obvious. Cupid stood differently, and when he looked at her, that was different too. He was still a ten year old boy, but he was a ten year old who could remember the millennia he had been that age.

"Thank you," he said, and it sounded curiously formal coming from such a young boy. He looked at Scarlett, smiled to himself as if in celebration of some private joke, and then disappeared as quickly as he had come.

"We should go after him," Aphrodite said. "He'll only go and get into trouble again."

"After you have undone what you did," Hephaestus insisted.

Aphrodite sighed and waved a hand vaguely in the direction of Cruces, Tavian and Scarlett. "There, it's done, are you happy now?"

"Our son is himself, your curse is gone, and your earlier one is broken," Hephaestus said. "How could I not be?" He nodded to Scarlett. "Farewell, and thank you, all of you."

He vanished, leaving Aphrodite there. The goddess looked at Scarlett, then at Cruces, before smiling to herself just momentarily. "Yes, I suppose I should say thank you. I have my son back at least. I wish you well, my dear, trying to sort this one out."

She didn't say more than that but vanished after Hephaestus. Scarlett found herself wondering what Aphrodite had meant. More than that, she found herself wondering if the goddess had truly removed her curse. How would she know? Would it just be a matter of what she felt?

Well, what did she feel? The all-encompassing love for Tavian was gone. Of that much, Scarlett was certain. Yet there was still something there when she looked at him, and Cruces... Scarlett had felt her attraction to him even when the curse was still in place. What did that mean? Did it mean that it was him she loved? Yet what Aphrodite had done to her had left Scarlett free to express what she felt for Tavian, and she wasn't willing to give that away

229

completely simply because she was herself again. In any case, how did she know what either of the men really felt? How much of *that* had been because of Aphrodite?

It seemed that getting rid of the curse had not solved everything. Scarlett sighed as she understood Aphrodite's parting words. Her life was going to get complex indeed before it became simple again. On the other hand, at least now, she could be certain that whatever she felt was her own feelings and not some spell. That was something.

Now she just had to work out exactly what she *did* feel.

Epilogue

Scarlett sat at home that night alone except for the servants at her parents' London house. Both Cruces and Tavian had tried to insist that Scarlett should not be alone given the potential danger posed by Lydia, but as Scarlett had pointed out, the only way to make absolutely sure that Lydia could not get near her would be to remain under their watch every hour of the day. Scarlett was not prepared to do that.

For one thing, she needed a certain amount of space in which to think about how things had turned out thanks to the various spells she had been under. She had felt love. It had been forced on her by immortal powers, but it had been love nonetheless, so deep and consuming that it had left no time for anything else. It had reduced Scarlett to something less than herself, making her into one of those foolish girls she so disliked having to spend time around at parties and functions.

Scarlett was not sure that she wanted to feel like that again, even as she knew that somewhere under her denial, feelings lurked in a knot that was almost impossible to sort out. Cruces, Tavian… there was even a small, lingering thread of grief for Rothschild's passing, despite the fact that all the love she had felt for him came from the bow. Though maybe that was just that they had been connected so strongly. Honestly, who would willingly welcome love like that?

"Love can be difficult, can't it?"

Scarlett looked up to see Hephaestus standing in the drawing room of her home. She had not seen him arrive, which suggested that he had done so without any kind of spectacle. Scarlett found herself looking around for Aphrodite, worried that something had gone wrong, or that the immortals intended something else unpleasant for her.

232

"Relax," Hephaestus said. "My wife is not here. She has what she wants and so has no further interest in you for now."

"But you do?" Scarlett asked.

Hephaestus smiled. "It merely occurred to me that we did not truly reward our champion for bringing back Cupid's bow. Oh, Aphrodite removed her curse, but merely taking away something that she had already inflicted hardly counts as a reward."

Hephaestus wanted to reward her? Scarlett's hopes rose as she started to consider what she might be able to ask for. Would the Greek god be able to tell her where Gordon was? Would he be able to return Cecilia? Would he...

"Remember that we cannot intervene in mortal affairs," Hephaestus said. "Still, the gift I have in mind is one you might find useful."

He held out a hand and the air above it seemed to shimmer. A golden goblet appeared, falling into Hephaestus' outstretched hand.

"I don't understand," Scarlett admitted. She could feel the power coming from the object, but even so, why would she need a golden cup.

"Any liquid placed in this cup turns into ambrosia," Hephaestus explained. "Drink from it, and you will be an immortal."

"But that's..." For several seconds, Scarlett was simply lost for words. She had done no more than find one object, yet here Hephaestus was, offering her eternal life. "It's too much. I don't deserve it."

"You returned my son's immortality," Hephaestus said. "This seems like the most fitting way to repay that."

Scarlett's brow furrowed. "So why did you not simply use the cup to make Cupid immortal again when his bow was taken? You could have done that, surely?"

"I could," Hephaestus agreed, "but then would my son have been the same? He would have been immortal, but he would not have had his powers."

"I've been on the receiving end of some of those powers through the bow," Scarlett pointed out.

"True, but do you think what he does is all bad? Do you think Zeus would have allowed him to continue this

234

long if that were the case? Cupid and my wife play many tricks, but love... love is vital. Love is powerful. Humans need it almost as much as they need air to breathe, even if they do not know it. It is something to be cherished and protected."

"Yet you and Aphrodite still argue," Scarlett pointed out.

Hephaestus spread his hands. "I did not say that love made things perfect. I did not even say it made them easy. Yet I can tell you that, for all Aphrodite and I have between us, I will never regret my love for her. But that is for another day. What do you plan to do with my gift, Scarlett? Will you drink from it at once? Both of the young men vying for your affections have the potential to live a long, long time."

Scarlett thought carefully. It was true that Cruces had lived thousands of years already, and the fey appeared to be effectively immortal, so Tavian might do the same. To match them, drinking from the cup seemed like the natural thing to do, yet she did not. Not yet. Being human was enough for Scarlett right then.

"That is good enough for now," the immortal said. "Living this long is not always ideal. The cup is yours to keep in any case. I trust that you will use it wisely, and judge the right moment to drink from it for yourself. Now, I must go. No doubt my son is up to something."

Scarlett started to thank Hephaestus, but the Greek god was gone, leaving the cup hanging in midair just long enough for Scarlett to catch it and place it carefully on the mantelpiece. The quest for the bow was over at least.

Too many things weren't though. Gordon was still missing, and Rothschild was no longer around to tell them where he had been taken. Cecilia was somewhere in the lands of the fey. The Order still clearly wanted the Devices, and Scarlett was in personal danger now. She did not think that Lydia would stop easily. She might even learn how to control the shadows that had almost overwhelmed her in the cave. That would be a frightening thought.

Though somehow, it was also a comforting one. It meant that Scarlett's life was not about to become anything normal in the near future. It meant that she would have the adventure of trying to deal with things most young women her age could not begin to comprehend. She also had to work out where Cruces and Tavian fit into her life, if they did at all.

All in all, it looked like there were going to be plenty of adventures ahead for her.

Steampunk Scarlett's adventures continues in
Book 3 of Steampunk Scarlett

Ethereal Devices

2012

237

From Bestselling Author Kailin Gow comes

FADE

"My name is Celestra Caine. I am seventeen years old, which makes me a senior at Richmond High. I never thought this would happen to me, but it has… I'm one of those people you see every day, go to school with, remember seeing at the supermarket or the mall, and then one day you don't hear about them any longer. They're gone, and eventually, you forget them."

From Bestselling Author Kailin Gow comes

DESIRE

A Dystopian world where everyone's future is planned out for them at age 18…whether it is what a person desires or not. Kama is about to turn 18 and she thinks her Life's Plan will turn out like her boyfriend's and friend's – as they desired. But when she glimpse a young man who can communicate with her with his thoughts and knows her name…a young man with burning blue eyes and raven hair, who is dressed like no other in her world, she is left to question her Life's Plan and her destiny.

Excerpt from Kailin Gow's Dystopian Series

DESIRE

Book 1

kailin gow

240

Prologue

Perfection. That was how best to described the day. Blue skies with the hint of lilac and buttercream, fat fluffy white clouds gliding by added to the beautiful day. It was the perfect way to end a sunny school day. With my hand nestled warmly in Liam's, I walked at his side, my face tilted up to the sun, my nostrils breathing in the fresh air that smelled like Spring lavenders and fresh linen. The fragrant air made me think of Spring formals, garden parties, and outdoor barbeques. The day could not be more enjoyable if it'd been planned that way. If I had not grown up anywhere else besides the state of Arcadia, I would have thought this was the way it always was everywhere.

School had gone well, tests and exams had been passed with flying colors and the birds seemed to be singing perfectly. Like every day in Arcadia.

As we approached Nellie's Diner, I caught a glimpse of myself in a store window and was pleased with the reflection I saw. My long blonde hair cascaded down my back, freshly brushed and tidy. The lustrous locks fluttered in the breeze in a way that always made Liam smile, and it all added a bounce to my step.

That morning I'd chosen to wear my pale green smock dress, the one that he always complimented me on.

"That dress sure does make those hazel eyes of yours pop," he'd always say.

Always told I was a pretty girl, I never really believed it until Liam and I began dating in high school. At his side I felt beautiful. Was it his striking features that enhanced my sense of beauty or was it simply the look of adoration I saw in his eyes every time he looked at me that made me feel so beautiful?

"How'd you do on your math test?" he asked.

Though I'd always managed to get good grades, I never failed to get nervous and edgy when test time came around. "I think it went well," I said, smiling at him and adoring him all the more for the concern he always showed for me and my studies.

"I think I pretty much aced that History exam this morning," he said with pride.

He was so handsome, his fair curls so angelic. It never failed to amaze me how sweet, kind and generous he could be. A guy as handsome as Liam could easily break a thousand hearts, yet he was thoughtful and considerate in the way he treated every woman he met, and he was particularly attentive, loving and caring with me.

"Maybe my Life's Plan should have been to become a history professor," he added as he opened the door to the diner, his bright blue eyes twinkling with laughter and amusement.

I shared his hope and promise, and questioned what my own Life's Plan would be. With my eighteenth birthday quickly approaching, I would know all too soon. It was as though I had been waiting all my life to find out what my Life Plan would be. All of us under the age of eighteen waited with anxiety and anticipation to find out what our Life's Plan held: our profession, who we would marry, where we would live, and how many children we would have. It would all be written in our Life's Plan.

"Kama! Liam," Sarah called from across the crowded diner. "Hey, you love birds, over here."

243

I couldn't count the number of eyes that watched us as we made our way to our table. We'd been voted the best-looking couple in school for two years, and some even said we were the most attractive couple in town. Some claimed I had pale violet highlights that shined in the bright summer sun, though I can't say I ever really noticed them myself. Some even hinted at the added degree of elegant glamour my recently fashioned bangs gave me. Others were envious of what they call my porcelain skin.

It was all flattering, but it was also incredibly embarrassing. I felt scrutinized and watched all the time. Added to this was the expectation that Liam and I would soon marry. The thought both pleased and pressured me. I'd known Liam since I could remember, but the pressure to marry was sometimes difficult to swallow. I wanted to do this on my own terms, not by everyone's expectations.

"After you." Liam gestured to the booth.

"Have you been waiting long?" I asked Sarah as I slid in.

"Just long enough to down one of these." She held up a tall, long glass of soda then turned to Liam. "You know, I was thinking, next week we could do the party down by the lake if the weather holds up."

"I'm famished. Have you ordered yet?"

"Two mini burgers with coleslaw and a mammoth burger with fries for Liam."

"Thanks," Liam said, obviously anticipating the great meal to come.

"So, what do you think? Sarah asked him.

"I had thought about that, too. Streamers on the trees, flowers everywhere, and maybe even a live band? Or we could do something elegant and classy at my place. The grounds are beautiful this time of year with everything in bloom."

"I think she would really love that."

"I just love how you guys go about planning my birthday party as if I wasn't even there."

"It's as close to a surprise party as we can get. You always guess what we're up to anyway." Sarah pointed her straw at me for emphasis.

"But the night of my birthday is the same as the Arcades last game of the season."

"That's if they make it to the finals." Liam seemed unconcerned with the turn out of the evening.

"They always make it," Sarah added.

"Even if they do, everybody's going to want to come celebrate Kama's birthday."

It was just like Liam to be so optimistic. I suddenly thought of the secret wedding plans I'd conjured up for us. As annoying as the pressure to marry could sometimes be, the thought that marrying Liam might not be in my Life's Plan often scared me to death.

"That's pushing it a bit, don't you think?" I knew I was popular at school, but for the student body to skip the Arcades' victory party for my eighteenth birthday wasn't likely to happen.

"Look," Sarah said with finality. "The game is at two, will probably end before five, everyone will celebrate 'til seven and then they can all slide on over to our party for eight. Voila. It's all settled and everyone is happy."

I tried to concentrate on what she was saying, but I felt every sense in my body awaken to something I'd never felt before. It was electric, almost painful. Was this what closing in on my eighteenth birthday felt like?

No, it was more than just that. I stared out the window, looking for the source of my sudden distraction. The feeling intensified until the conversation between Sarah and Liam was completely blotted out and all that existed was that odd sensation.

"Kama, did you hear what I said?"

I pulled my gaze away with difficulty and concentrated on Sarah who wove a lilac colored sheet of paper at me

I knew what it meant and instantly felt that jolt of envy. Having turned eighteen a few weeks back, she'd finally received her Life's Plan.

"I finally got word from the Committee. Can you believe it? I hold in my hand my Life's Plan."

"And you managed to hold that bit of information back this long?" I said, teasing her.

"I love you and want this birthday to be special for you, but now that everything is practically settled, we can talk about *moi*."

"So, what does the future hold for *toi*?"

247

Before she could answer, the waitress arrived with our order.

"Everything looks delicious as usual. Thank you," Sarah said with a quick, polite but dismissive smile. She was eager to tell us about her Life's Plan and it showed.

Beaming with pride, she pulled out her electronic pad, inserted the small chip she'd received from the Committee and turned the screen to Liam and me.

Ignoring the plate of hot food before me, I read through the introduction, though I basically knew it all. She came from the affluent Diamond Suburbs, was the only child to Mick and Fay Murray who both happened to work on the very Committee she'd just received notice from.

"Okay, so you guys already know that part," Sarah said as she guided the page further down. "Here's the interesting part."

I smiled as I envisioned the life that had been plotted out for her. She was to attend Arcadia University where she would meet her future husband in the Elite Society. Both would go on to work for the Committee and live in the Diamond Suburb.

248

"Oh, Sarah. I'm so excited for you." I finally picked up my little burger and sank my teeth into it.

"I knew you'd be. This is exactly what I wanted. Exactly what I was hoping for."

"Do you know how lucky you are to receive a Life's Plan that is just as you wanted it?"

"I know. I never would have thought."

I turned to Liam who'd sat silently through the exchange, his mammoth burger almost half gone. A wistful smile warmed his face as he looked at me. That look of love that came so often still warmed me just as much as it did on our very first date. He slid his hand around my waist and pulled me closer and I knew where his mind had wandered to; his own Life's Plan.

He was set to marry a girl he'd known all his life. It could hardly be anyone else but me. Everyone agreed we were the perfect match. He would someday take his dad's place as Governor of Arcadia, but would start at the Committee. He, too, was slated to live in the luxurious suburb of Diamond.

How many times had he told me his Life's Plan had to include me? Countless. And every time he did, my heart raced a little faster. Life would indeed be perfect; a beautiful home in an exclusive neighborhood, a loving and gorgeous husband, and my best friend living nearby. What more could I hope for?

I couldn't resist leaning into him for a warm snuggle. He wrapped his arms around me, kissed my forehead and chuckled in that soft way he had when he knew I was feeling amorous.

"Cool it, you guys," Sarah snapped. "I'm still here, in case you hadn't noticed. Besides, this is my Life's Plan we're happy about, remember? You'll have your chance in a few weeks, Kama."

Yes, I wanted to scream. And I hoped I wouldn't have to wait long. While some people waited weeks, as Sarah had, many got their Life's Plan within days of their eighteenth. No doubt mine would greatly resemble Sarah's and Liam's. We were basically cut from the same cloth, even if our childhoods were slightly different, and our destinies were bound to include one another.

The sensation returned again, drawing my attention away from the table and pulling me out of the diner like a magnet. I looked out the window, looking for the source of my distraction.

Across the street, simply standing there, tall, dark and strangely out of place, was a young man of such intensity, the hair on my arms rose. He was like no other man I'd ever seen, confident, sure and so attractive in his gloom. His fashion sense was from another world, or at the very least from another town.

While the occasional blue jean was seen here and there, most young men of Arcadia wore stylish and elegant slacks. But this intruder dared to wear not only jeans, but black jeans that seemed to have seen their share of battle. Instead of a shirt, he wore a dark leather tunic that added to his mystique and aura of danger.

I was drawn to him in a way I'd never thought possible. It was magnetic. I felt my heart quicken and my pulse race. He was like a warrior straight out of those romantic fantasy novels I'd heard about. Extremely handsome, a bit exotic with his tan skin and jet-black hair.

251

But his sapphire eyes held mine in a gaze that spoke lifetimes.

Kama, the desired one.

My fork stopped midway to my mouth. I froze as the strange and dark voice entered my mind. I glanced at Sarah. Happily chomping on her burger, she had not heard a thing.

Glancing sidelong at Liam, I could see he had not heard anything either.

I have found you, yet again...

What? Me? Who are you? What is this? Where was that voice coming from?

Him.

I forced the coleslaw into my mouth before the others noticed my sudden odd behavior, but I almost choked on it. When I finally managed to swallow it down, I turned to Liam.

"I think I just saw Tula across the street," I said as I laid down my fork and prepared to rise. "I owe her two dollars, so I'll run out to give it back to her."

252

He stood, and while he looked completely perplexed by my sudden need to leave the diner, he said nothing.

I hurried out and headed in the direction of the mysterious man with raven hair. Breathless before I even began to run across the street, I felt an urgent need to meet this man. But I could see before hitting the curb that he'd already disappeared.

My disappointment surprised me, as if I'd missed something important, something that could change my life. My heart felt heavy as I looked up and down the street. There wasn't even a trace of him until I arrived at the very spot I'd seen him.

A perfect deep purple orchid. It had to come from him. No orchid of such color grew in Arcadia. It was the only proof I was not completely going nuts. He had been here. I had seen him. This mysterious man with the burning blue eyes was here and knew my name. Who was he?

Want to Know More about *Steampunk Scarlett Series*, Author Insight, Author Appearance, Contests and Giveaways?

Join the Kailin Gow's Official Facebook Fan Page at:

http://www.facebook.com/KailinGowBooks

Talk to Kailin Gow, the bestselling author of over 80 distinct books for all ages at:

http://kailingow.wordpress.com

and

on Twitter at: @kailingow

CPSIA information can be obtained at www.ICGtesting.com
Printed in the USA
BVOW011741220112

281126BV00001B/125/P